THE GIRL AT C

For Jo

Alex Rushton

Best wishes

Alex Rushton

SCRIPTORA

Published in Great Britain 2019 by

SCRIPTORA

25 Summerhill Road

London N15 4HF

in association with SWWJ (The Society of Women

Writers & Journalists)

www.swwj.co.uk

ISBN 978-0-9500591-3-6

Printed and bound by Witley Press Hunstanton PE36 6AD

For Trevor with gratitude and love.

Special thanks and much appreciation go to my editor, Mary Rensten, for her sound advice, continuing encouragement and insightful comments on this manuscript.

Thanks to my friends at Walton Wordsmiths, especially Pat Jones, Shelley Miller, Guy Blythman and Howard Schaverien for their helpful feedback and support.

Thanks, also, to Pat Alderman for her proofreading.

CHAPTER 1

January 1986
Conway Place, Brandon Wood, North London

Wrapped in her old blue woollen coat, her arms crossed against her chest, Cathy paced the corridor of her flat; she shivered and looked at her watch. I hope Ricardo comes soon, she said to herself, I really need this boiler fixed. She drew her coat tighter. It was time she threw it away, she knew that, it reminded her too much of Blake; even the smell of it brought back a rush of memories of the awesome time they spent together. Oh, pull yourself together, Cathy! Stop being nostalgic. An independent, single woman in charge of her life, that's what I am now.

The doorbell rang and she swallowed hard, hesitating for a moment. Right, I'd better let him in. She opened the door and stood aside.

'Ricardo, good to see you again.'

'I have parts now, I get this morning, soon heater he work again.'

'Oh good, that's just what I want to hear.' She smiled at him. 'No more boiling kettles for bath water, and shivering.'

He held her gaze.

'It nice come here, see you, Cathy. So, nice lady, I do best job I can for you.'

'Thanks, I'm sure it will be very good.'

He followed her down the long, wide corridor to the kitchen and went straight to the boiler. He put his toolbox on the floor beside it. Cathy stood nearby with her back against a wall unit, her arms loose across her belly and her fingers linked, watching as he examined the boiler.

1

Soft black curls framed his handsome face; his mouth was generously curved and his nose arched, his skin olive and Mediterranean. When he glanced at her, smiling, his face lit up with brightness and warmth.

'Here the new valve,' he said, pulling it out of the toolbox; he stroked the shiny metal.

'Oh, good.'

He switched off the power to the boiler, opened it, pulled back the cover and unscrewed the protective rectangular metal plate.

'It not so cold here in kitchen.' He took off his scarf and put it over the back of a chair.

'No, I've had a fan heater on. I've another in the living room; they keep the frost away.'

'Is good.' He smiled at her again. 'You remember I tell you about my mother and my sister?'

'Yes, you said you live with them.'

'Last week I work two days only. I take my mother to hospital; she has bad hip, cannot walk.' He pointed to his hip. 'I order wheelchair for her…'

Ricardo chatted on, but Cathy was no longer listening. She was thinking about how nice it would be if there was someone caring about her, sharing her life, her intimate moments, wondering if she would ever be ready for someone else…

'So I wait for delivery. He come very late, so I no can work. Then I take mother to hospital, for fitting.'

'You are a very good son… Look, would you like some tea or coffee?'

'So kind, Cathy.' He glanced at her, his brown eyes warm and trusting, 'Yes, coffee please, but I try be quick for you.'

She hesitated.

'No need, I'm here all day today anyway. In fact it's nice to have your company.' Cathy walked across the kitchen and turned on the kettle. 'Sometimes I'm all alone and I see no one.' Fool! Why did I say that? she asked herself. I want to be upbeat. I don't want to give him the wrong impression, to think I'm pathetic, or worse, lonely.

'You have child, no? I see toys on floor, pictures on walls.'

'Yes, I have a son, but I collect him from school much later. And today is my day off.'

'You work?'

'Yes, just part-time.'

She hugged her coat close, with her back resting against the sink while the kettle boiled.

'What you do?'

'Administration, paperwork... in a solicitor's office.'

'You like work?'

'It's OK.'

The kettle bubbled and steam rose from the spout. She made the coffee and passed the mug to him.

'You very nice lady.' Their eyes met, his expression open and genuine. He took a sip, put the mug on the worktop, turned and continued working, his hands deep in the mechanics of the boiler.

'You no like on your own?'

'Sometimes, not always.'

There was a long silence; he glanced at her briefly.

'You not have nice man?'

'No, my husband... he's not with us anymore.'

Ricardo stopped for a moment and turned towards her. He took a gulp of coffee and studied her closely. 'I sorry, very sorry – so your son he no have father.'

'No. My son was a baby when... he never met his father.'

He shook his head and frowned, his expression pained.

'I no have father. He bad man, my mother leave him, took me and sister. My mother always alone.'

3

'I'm sorry, but she's fortunate to have a good son like you.'

'My mother, she very good cook. She make best Trenette al Pesto in the whole of Toscana.' He kissed his thumb and forefinger. 'Also Linguine allo Scoglio, she make very good.'

'Pasta dishes?'

'Yes, pasta.'

'I see.'

'I do everything for my mother. I try to make her happy. Always, she knows.'

Ricardo replaced the boiler cover and clicked it into position. He turned the control knob and there was a 'whoosh' as it fired up.

He listened for a moment then said, 'It OK now. Like new.'

'That's a relief, but it's not very old anyway. The previous owner installed the central heating only a couple of years before I moved in.'

'The rest of boiler, he good. Now new valve, all very good. Soon it be warm here, you can take coat off.'

Digging into his toolbox, Ricardo picked out a small card.

'Here my name and telephone. I put this on side here... on boiler.' He showed her where. 'Then, if problems, you call.'

'Oh, yes please, that's helpful.'

He peeled off the paper backing, stuck the card in place and wrote that day's date on it.

'Next I test radiators.'

'No hurry,' Cathy smiled. 'Finish your coffee, then I'll show you where they all are.'

'Thank you. You very kind.' He looked at his hands. 'It a little dirt. You mind I wash hands?'

'No, of course not, use the kitchen sink.'

He walked to the sink. Finished, Ricardo put his tools away in his box.

'You my last customer today and it only early. I have free afternoon then later I go to friend to play mandolin.'

'Oh, are you good?'

'I play for much years and I write and sing also. It remind me of home.'

'Come and sit down through here, it's more comfortable.' She led the way, encouraging him into the living room. Why did I say that? Is this a good idea? she asked herself. Am I that desperate for male company?

'This big room,' he said, glancing around. 'Soon they be warm.' He put his hand on the base of a radiator. 'Yes, it come warm soon. These curtains, they thick, keep heat in,' he said as he stroked them between his thumb and forefinger. 'This flat, big rooms and tall.' He pointed to the ceiling. 'How many flats?'

'Nine, three on each floor. The block of flats was built in the 1950s, it's unusual really for the time, solid, big hallways, wide staircases. It's so much better than most of the rubbish that was built then.'

'Here on first floor good for keep heat in, but big windows also. Much sun but heat, he go out.'

'Yes, I haven't noticed that I suppose.'

'How long you live here?'

'I moved to Brandon Wood just before my son was born.'

'You like?'

'Yes, I do. It's convenient for the school and my work; they're both nearby and the shops are just round the corner. The Grand Union Canal is about a half hour's drive away. I like walking there.'

'And you have park outside.'

'Yes, I take my son there.' She smiled at him. 'Where do you live?'

'We many years in Stanmore. But for shopping my mother she like Edgware, she buy many foods for her cooking.'

Looking around, he noticed a framed photograph of Cathy and baby Jason in a prime position on a set of drawers and went to it. 'Your son, very nice boy. How old now?'

'He's four, five in April.' She tidied away some of the toys from the floor into a basket. 'Please, sit.' She gestured towards an armchair.

An hour later, he had told her about his early life in Florence, the birth of his younger sister, his uncle's farm, his medley of mandolin tunes, travelling to North London, his plumbing course in Bermondsey and his stamp collecting. During the course of his reminiscing he had relaxed; he was now sunk comfortably into the chair, his feet propped on the footstool. She listened attentively throughout, impressed by his uninhibited genuineness and naive simplicity. She told him about her university days in Manchester, studying Combined Sciences, and her passion for rock climbing. He'd shown a real interest and the conversation flowed freely and spontaneously. His voice was soft and lilting and easy to listen to, despite his convoluted English. Gosh, this must be the first time I've sat in this room and had a happy relaxed conversation with a man since Jason was born, she thought. And it feels good. There's something about him that reminds me of Blake; what is it? Yes, I think it's the way his feet are crossed on the footstool, but Ricardo is wearing shoes and Blake's feet were always bare. I loved his sockless feet. I remember him sitting right there reading the newspaper. I'd catch his eye and he'd smile tenderly at me and his love made me feel so complete. She peeled off her coat and put it on the back of the sofa.

'You warm now?' he asked.

'Yes.' She gulped, her eyes filling with tears.

'You sad?'

'This coat… I wore it the first time I met my husband… it's stupid really.'

He frowned and cocked his head to one side. 'Not stupid.'

Cathy sat tightly on her settee, her knees curled up beneath her.

'I never lonely because I have mother and sister… ' He frowned suddenly. 'I hate think of you lonely.'

'I have my son…'

'You very beautiful woman, many men want be with you, to hug you.'

'I wouldn't know… it's been a long time.'

'I hug you, if you want.'

Without hesitation he got up and sat beside her on the sofa. With genuine warmth he embraced her in an affectionate hug. He held her softly and securely for a long moment. The warmth of his body and the smell of him, earthy smells, aroused something in her that had been dormant and repressed for a long time. She felt the rise and fall of his chest, the reassuring physical closeness she had missed so much. It had been so long. She took a prolonged and deep breath and relaxed. There was an instinctive sexual quickening within her, a slackening then tightening of her belly. How long must I wait, she wondered? These feelings… no… I mustn't be irresponsible… but… Is this the right time? Is it too soon? Will the time ever be right? Oh, what the hell… I am a living, breathing woman after all, not a dried-up prune. Feeling his cheek on hers, she searched for his mouth with her lips.

CHAPTER 2

'I don't like to think too far into the future,' said Holly, fingering the handle of her teacup with her immaculately manicured fingers. 'As long as they keep giving me pay rises, I'll keep going.'

'You won't find it too much, taking on another three shops?' asked Cathy.

Holly finished off her thickly-cut cheese and tomato sandwich, dabbed her mouth and wiped her hands on a tissue from her skirt pocket.

'No, it's just more of the same. More people to train, of course, but teaching twenty-five is about the same as teaching five, darling. I'll just get my PA to hire a larger room.' She sipped her tea.

'You'll be on the Board of Directors soon.'

Holly smiled wryly.

'Funny you should mention that, my manager made a quip about it, just the other day.'

Cathy looked over at Jason, who was sitting close up to the television, engrossed in a Tom and Jerry cartoon. An empty plate surrounded by crumbs lay on the carpet beside him.

'If you do you'll have even less time to spend with George,' she said.

'Hmm,' Holly mused. 'George is always travelling. He telephones every day when he's in the country, we meet whenever we can, but, well, sometimes we're pretty much like ships passing in the night.'

'Wouldn't you like to settle down with him?'

Holly sighed.

'It's difficult, you know, Cathy... we are both career people, time just flies.' She reached over and put her plate on the low table beside the armchair. 'Very nice sandwich, darling, but if you could cut the bread a bit thinner next time I won't feel like a codfish.'

'Oh, sorry.'

The doorbell rang.

'Are you expecting anyone?' asked Holly.

Cathy looked at her watch.

'Midday on Saturday... no one. No idea who it is. I'll go and see.' She went to the front door and opened it.

Ricardo, beaming, thrust a big bunch of yellow daffodils right at her. His black hair was slicked back and he was dressed in a smart blue jacket and patent leather black shoes.

'For beautiful Cathy. I bring flowers, I think of you all the time.' His expression was full of happy expectation, his eyes sparkling. 'And of our future together.'

'I... I... thanks, Ricardo, but not now, thank you,' stammered Cathy. She stepped back.

'Cathy, I want you have flowers for our loving time together – very special.'

Cathy sensed Holly's presence just behind her.

'I'm sorry, but I think you don't understand me.'

'No understand? Yes, I understand.' He lowered the daffodils slightly and looked at Holly. 'This your friend? Then my friend also. I want know your friend. Friend of Cathy is friend of mine.'

'What's going on?' asked Holly.

'Nothing... it's OK,' mumbled Cathy.

'My mother she says, beautiful lady with broken boiler I meet her and her family and friends for happy together.'

'Stop... please stop,' urged Cathy, feeling herself go hot; she ran a finger under the collar of her shirt. 'I'm sorry,' she pushed the door closed a bit, 'I didn't mean to give you the wrong impression or false expectations. But it's not possible... not now... not ever. Please forgive me.'

'I no understand? I bring flowers.'

He thrust them towards her again.

Cathy turned away and lowered her head. 'Please, Ricardo, goodbye.'

She pushed the door to close it but felt resistance as Ricardo pushed from the other side.

'Cathy, no mistake, we speak, you see... Cathy!'

She put the whole weight of her body against the door and Holly joined in. Soon it closed tight with a reassuring click. Cathy leaned back against it, her heart pounding, and closed her eyes tight.

The doorbell rang, then stopped. Then it rang again, and again and again as Ricardo kept his finger on the bell-push. Cathy put her hands to her ears.

'Here, let me,' said Holly.

Cathy shook her head and in an urgent whisper said, 'No.'

'Let me, I can do this,' insisted Holly.

'Do what?'

'Make him go.'

'OK, you try then.'

Cathy moved aside and Holly opened the door halfway, still holding it firmly in position with one hand.

'Look, whatever's happened, it's a mistake, OK? Now go back to your mother and give her the flowers, I'm sure she'll love them.'

'But... '

'Please leave Cathy alone, she's not well. Now, there's a good man, let that be the end of it. Goodbye.'

Holly slammed the door shut. Looking intently at each other, they listened as Ricardo shouted Cathy's name repeatedly, then some minutes later to the echo of his footsteps as they faded away down the stairs.

'My goodness,' said Holly. 'What on earth have you been up to?'

Before Cathy could reply Jason tugged on her skirt. 'Finished now,' he said, 'I'm still hungry.'

Cathy took a few deep breaths.

'What, after all those sandwiches?'

'Yes.' Jason stared at her intently. 'Mummy, why is your face all red?'

Cathy put her hands on her cheeks; she felt them burning hot and took some more deep breaths.

'Why don't you go and play with your abacus and I'll get you some chocolate pudding as a special treat.'

'Yay! Then we'll play football in the park?'

'It's a bit cold for that. Maybe later, darling.'

Jason skipped off to his bedroom; Cathy swallowed hard.

Back in the living room she switched off the television.

'He tears at my heartstrings,' she whispered and wiped away a tear. 'I'm so confused. He doesn't have a Daddy, for God's sake. He needs a dad to play football with. We're in the park and he tries to join in games with other kids with their dads. It's really hard. I see how the other parents look at me... sometimes I think they're hostile... I can feel it.'

'I think you might be over-reacting, although it can't be easy being a single mum.'

'It's not, it's bloody difficult. I feel like an outcast.'

Holly turned her head; there was a repetitive knocking from within the flat.

'What's that noise? My nerves must be on edge.'

'It's OK, just Jason playing with his abacus. He puts his wooden blocks on top of each other as he counts the beads on the track.'

Holly looked back at Cathy. 'Here isn't a good place to talk.'

'No, let's go to the kitchen.'

Having turned the corner at the end of the long corridor

11

and gone into the kitchen, they settled into the aluminium chairs at the rectangular wooden table. Jason's booster seat was clamped high on to one chair; on the table in front of it was a blue plastic cup with a Mickey Mouse printed on it and brightly coloured Lego blocks.

'So, what's with this Ricardo then, Cathy? Who is he?' Holly's eyes were sharp and inquiring as she held Cathy's gaze.

'Do you have to ask me these awkward questions?' Cathy snapped.

'I've known you for over twenty years and I've just saved you from him so I think you owe it to me to tell me.'

Cathy sighed and, her elbows on the table, put her face in her hands.

'If you must know, he's a plumber.'

'Your plumber?'

'He was, until… '

Cathy uncovered her face and looked away.

'The poor guy was beside himself. He looks quite cute. But really, Cathy.'

'Don't criticise me, Holly. I've been on my own for five years, no, more than five years now. No intimacy, no nothing,' she said sharply. 'A whole six years, imagine that.'

'Yes, that must be very difficult… '

'You've no idea what that's like.' Cathy forced back tears. 'Your life is so simple and straightforward with George. You know you'll see him again soon, spend the night together… '

Holly drew in her breath sharply.

'Well, you're wrong; it's not actually that easy. Our relationship takes a lot of patience and negotiation, but anyway, forget about George, this is about you. You need a man in your life, that's screamingly obvious. So you'd better go and get one.' Holly crossed her arms. She had that resolute look that Cathy knew well. 'Now, what about the men you meet at work?'

'I don't meet anyone at work, only pensioners writing their wills and the occasional couple wanting conveyancing done. I've not met one suitable guy at work... and believe me I have noticed every single male who's walked into the office.'

'What about the solicitor you work for – Maurice, isn't it? You like him. He's got divorced, hasn't he?'

'Yes, he has, and now he's shacked up with some floozy half his age.'

Holly rhythmically tapped her fingers on the table and looked out of the window, deep in thought. 'Well, there is Ricardo… at least you fancied him.'

'He's lovely but I'd always be in competition with his mother. And I'd lose.' She shook her head. 'It was a big mistake.'

'All right, not him then. We have to find you someone though; let's make a checklist.' She clicked open her slick, bronze leather handbag and took out a silver pen and small spiral-bound notebook. 'What kind of man are you looking for?'

'It's a bit clinical this, isn't it? I'm not choosing a refrigerator. People are supposed to have wonderful chemistry and fall in love, aren't they?'

'Only in the movies. Now let's be realistic and pragmatic. Your ideal man, please.' Holly had the pen poised over the notebook, ready to write.

'Oh, I don't know, just someone I'll like. It's difficult because I remember... ' She bit her lower lip and looked away. 'He's also got to get on with Jason. Take him to things like the dads' and kids' weekend. Someone who will be considerate and reliable.' She sighed. 'I suppose it's not realistic to expect a wild romance or deep love as well.'

They sat in silence for a while. Holly looked at her

13

inquisitively.

'What is it?' asked Cathy.

'I wish you'd tell me,' said Holly softly.

'Tell you what?'

'About Jason's father. About what happened?'

Cathy looked pensively out of the window for a few moments. She turned and gave Holly a hard stare. 'I don't want to talk about it.' She turned back and looked out of the window again. It's easier if I don't even think about it, she thought. If I just try to live for today. I can't think about what ifs. How things might have been, it's too painful, I might go mad.

'OK, sorry.' Holly sucked in her lips and looked at her watch, tore the piece of paper with the list from her notebook and put it on the table in front of Cathy. 'Now, look closely at this and add to it if you can think of any other qualities your ideal man needs. I'm sorry, darling, I have to go. I have a hair appointment, colour and blow-dry.'

Cathy shrugged. 'Your hair looks fine to me. How good does it have to be?'

Holly stood up; as she pushed her chair back it scraped on the linoleum flooring. Cathy followed her into the hallway. Holly slipped on her stilettos and unhooked her Gucci jacket from the wall, slinging it over her forearm.

'Now about you: I think, as a first stage, you should join a dating agency. Agreed?'

Cathy shrugged. 'I suppose so, why not.'

'I'll check out which is the best, leave it to me. I like doing investigations like this, I'm in my element. When we get the paperwork you fill it in and we'll take it from there. But for goodness sake, keep your hands off them; don't jump into bed on the first date, however horny you feel!'

Cathy gave a mock salute. 'Yes, ma'am!'

She heard Jason calling from his bedroom, 'Mummy,

where's my chocolate pudding?'

CHAPTER 3

Spotting Cathy sitting in a quiet corner of the empty bijou café, Holly walked briskly over to her.

'Hello, darling,' Holly said as she pecked Cathy on both cheeks, took off her tailored coat and settled onto the settee opposite.

'Good to see you, Holly.'

In front of them there was a low pine table; in the centre a single red rose stood in a cut glass vase. Soft music played in the background.

'That reminds me of romance.' Holly looked at the rose, bent over and smelled it. 'Roses in March, no wonder the coffee in here is so expensive.'

'It doesn't smell, does it?'

'No, of course not. What do you expect? It's March.' Holly sat back. 'Anyway, you're lucky to have such a nice café just round the corner from your flat.' She smiled at Cathy. 'I'm so pleased to see you. It's difficult talking on the phone with Jason in the background, not that I think he'd pay any attention to our conversation but, anyway, I'm here.'

'Was the journey OK?'

'Yes, surprisingly, it was. Hardly any traffic all the way from Hampstead, but then we're not in the rush hour.'

'Great.'

'So, what were they like, this first batch? I've been thinking about you and dying to know.' She probed Cathy with her piercing grey eyes.

'So you want me to dive straight in with all the gory details?'

'That's right; I'm ready to listen.'

'Look, are you happy here? It's a beautiful day, we

16

could sit outside if you like, we've both got coats and hats.'

'No, darling, I'm fine here. It's more intimate and we won't be overheard. Also it's a bit cold outside for me.'

'OK, I'm easy.'

'So Jason's with a friend?'

'Yes, Barnie.' She looked at her watch. 'So I've got about an hour.'

'Now... ' Holly looked expectantly at Cathy.

'Well…' Cathy smiled coyly, twisting her wristwatch.

'Any good ones?' Holly winked. 'Come on, spill it. I know there's something.'

'They're a range, from appalling to hopeful.'

'There shouldn't have been any really duff ones in there, we made our criteria quite clear. Anyway, carry on. I want *every* gory detail.'

'Oh dear... how embarrassing.'

'Go on.'

'Well, the first one, Alex, was this sports-mad guy with enormous muscles bulging under his Nike T-shirt. He had a broad smile with even teeth, like soldiers. He goes to the gym every day and jogs every weekend. He said he'd take me with him but when I said I had a son he froze.'

Holly sighed. 'I gave clear instructions to the agency to screen out guys who don't like children.'

'And I confirmed it when their secretary phoned me.'

'I'm disappointed with them. I took a long time selecting Harrow Dating Agency. That Sandra sounded on the ball. People are so incompetent these days.'

'But it wasn't going to work anyway so we mutually agreed to cut the date short. After all, there was zero chemistry between us.'

'And number two?'

'Number two was worse. Josh, a geeky intellectual who was into astronomy and peered at me with beady little eyes through his professor-type specs. He wore a suit and cravat. Really, I began to think we were in the nineteenth century.' Cathy sniggered. 'He also had a plethora of nasal hair, which was a definite romantic turn-off.'

'Oh dear... what about number three? Was there a third one?'

'There was. Actually number three is possible.' She half-smiled, cautiously.

'Name?'

'Simon. Simon Scott, in fact.'

'Likes children?'

'Yes, he's divorced; they didn't have any children. But he says he really likes kids, that's the best bit. He's met Jason and they got on really well.' Cathy's eyes lit up.

'That's good.'

'I was so pleased and relieved, you couldn't imagine.'

'So why did he break up with his wife?'

'Well, it's quite complicated. Ask me something else first.'

A waitress in a starched white apron came up, put two glasses of iced water on the table, dipped her hand into her pocket and pulled out a pen and notebook.

'Can I take your order, please?'

They glanced at the menus.

'What do you think?' asked Holly.

'Not sure. I'm easy, something fresh.'

'Shall we go for the quiche and salad with coleslaw on the side? I think you had that last time, remember?'

'Yes, vaguely.'

'Two of those, please.' Holly passed the menus to the waitress and looked straight back at Cathy.

'So, what's his job?'

'He's in technical sales. Air-conditioning units; he's busiest in spring but takes orders all year. He's quite high up – some sort of manager, it seems.'

'So he's a good communicator then.'

'Yes, and very easy to be with.'

'Where does he live?'

'About half an hour's drive away, in Watford, so not too far.'

'How old is he?'

'Thirty-five.'

'Hmm, about seven years older. I suppose that's an acceptable age gap. Is he solvent?'

'Certainly seems to be.'

'Has he got his own home?'

'He did have but in this job he's on the road a lot, so at the moment he's based at his mother's house.'

'Oh dear, that doesn't sound very good. We don't want another Ricardo, do we?' She sat back for a moment and took a sip of water. 'Did he talk about his mother? Is she elderly and demanding?'

'I don't believe so; she's quite independent, goes on walking holidays with friends. This is really different. He's not like Ricardo at all.'

'It's a bit strange, isn't it?'

'Yes, but what the hell, he doesn't strike me as a mummy's boy.' Cathy leant forward, closed her eyes and sniffed the rose. 'You're right, there's no smell at all.'

'You haven't... ?'

'No, of course not,' said Cathy, frowning.

Holly put her glass down and sat forwards again.

'But you fancy him?'

'Yes, I do... not passionately. He's not sex on sticks exactly, but he's clean and respectable-looking in a metropolitan, city sort of way. He's quite nice-looking I think.'

The waitress came over and laid the table with cutlery and napkins. They waited until she'd left.

'So,' Holly mused. 'I know it's early days, but what do

19

you feel about him?'

'I like him… quite a lot. To be honest, there's just the hint of… well he's a bit smooth I suppose, but I don't want that to put me off if everything else is OK. Especially if he gets on with Jason.'

Holly looked up into a corner of the room for a moment, considering, then asked:

'What do you mean… smooth?'

'Well, he's well-groomed, a bit too well-groomed for me in fact, I like them a bit more, well, rugged I suppose.' She frowned. 'When we were in Harrow once – he likes shopping actually – I noticed him looking at his reflection in shop windows, but it only happened a couple of times and was very quick.'

'That's a relief; he didn't linger and comb his hair I hope.'

'No,' she hesitated, frowning again, 'but there was this other time.'

'What was that?'

'This may sound a bit stupid to you but one day I noticed, when he took off his jumper because it was hot in… Debenhams, if I remember right, that he carefully placed it round his shoulders and tied the arms over his chest. He took a very long time doing it.'

'What's wrong with that?'

'Nothing, except that when he turned round I could see the Yves Saint Laurent label, and I wondered if he'd done it deliberately.'

Holly gave a short laugh.

'Who would he be trying to impress… you? He should have read you better than that… or he's hopelessly image-conscious. If he is you may have a problem.'

Cathy shrugged. 'Yes, I think I may have been mistaken.'

The waitress placed the quiche and salad lunches on the

table. The quiche was on the large side and the salad was a riot of healthy colours: red tomatoes, green lettuce and grated carrot. On another plate were pats of butter and slices of wholemeal bread for them to share. Holly carefully unwrapped her napkin and put it on her lap.

'Nice that he can afford Yves Saint Laurent though.'

'Hmm... ' Cathy sucked in her lips and frowned.

They started on the lunch.

'Yum, this quiche is quite delicious. Especially the asparagus.'

'Yes, it's really good. I like the crumbly pastry.'

There was a pause in the conversation while they ate their lunch.

'Anyway, back to you, Cathy. So, what about his background, his divorce?'

'Well, it's rather sad.'

'Oh, why?'

'He was really open, explained it all so clearly to me.'

'What happened?'

'He was duped, basically.'

'OK, how?'

'Well, Simon bought a house and married his long-term girlfriend Amy, who moved in. They were together about six years. Then he went into a business partnership with another man called Derek.'

'What sort of business?'

There was a pause; Cathy finished her quiche and put down her knife and fork.

'They were selling cosmetics, shampoos, etc. to hotels. They bought them cheaply in bulk, from Czechoslovakia, and sold them at a high mark-up. They started by using Simon's garage as a mini warehouse.'

'Go on.'

'The business took off and Simon remortgaged his house to finance the expansion into larger premises.'

'And then?'

'It all seemed to be going well, then Amy left him and moved in with Derek. It was a terrible shock. Then, to top it all, Simon found out Derek had been embezzling money from the firm.'

'I see.'

'Poor Simon. After that his business collapsed and Simon's house was repossessed. The police tracked Derek down and he repaid most of the money to avoid a jail sentence.'

'And that's why Simon's living with his mother?'

'Yes, but it's also convenient. He plans to buy another house sometime.'

'So, he's now formally divorced?'

'Yes, he's been on his own about two years.'

'I see.'

Holly dabbed her mouth with a napkin and looked out of the window for a moment, her eyes fixed on some distant point.

'Does he come over to you as gullible?' she asked.

'No, not at all.'

'Hmm... '

'Why do you ask?'

'Just because of his background. He didn't pick up that he was being betrayed, by both of them in fact, both his business partner and his wife?'

'No, sadly.'

'He's coming to you with quite a bit of baggage. I'd prefer him to have an uncomplicated, clean kind of background if that's possible, at his age.'

'Come on, Holly. None of this was his fault. I suppose it would be more complicated if he had his own kids, but he hasn't so that's better.'

Holly thought for a moment. 'And when he was telling you all this was he embarrassed or ashamed or sad?'

'No, he just told me, looking me straight in the eye in a matter-of-fact way. I think he's philosophical about it all now.'

Holly frowned.

'What is it?' Cathy sat back and folded her arms.

Holly pursed her lips. 'I think I need to meet him, darling.'

'Yes, that's a good idea. I'm sure you'll like him.'

'Hmm... how often have you seen him?'

'A few times... well, about five times I suppose.'

'And what have you done together?'

'Just eating out mainly, getting to know each other. We had lunch in the *Rose and Crown* once, you know, the pub down the road on Duke Street. He likes pubs and the odd beer or lager. But don't worry, he's not a heavy drinker.'

'Good.'

'He also likes old windmills and stately homes. He took me to this privately owned property, near Ashridge Park, with a windmill. It was quite interesting really. He says he wants us to go to lots of places together.'

'So he drives?'

'Yep, he's got a Ford Escort.'

'You wouldn't take him rock climbing?'

'No, I can't think he'd like that. I haven't suggested it.' Cathy sat back, looked at Holly and frowned. 'Look, you're very suspicious.'

'Well, I guess a single guy of thirty-five must have a history.'

'I've no reason to doubt him.'

Holly put her hand up and called over the waitress. 'Could I have a white coffee, please.' She caught Cathy's eye. 'Cathy?'

'No, water is fine for me.'

'Anyway, you said he'd met Jason?'

'Yes. I was very unsure about the timing but I thought I

ought to find out if Jason liked him. If he didn't it would be hopeless from the start.'

'So how did it go?'

'We met him in the park opposite the flat, and I introduced him as Mummy's new friend. Simon bought him a present, a football, which he knew is Jason's favourite game. It's a good way of getting him on side I guess. They kicked it around almost immediately.'

A group of smart young people came into the café, bringing in a waft of cold air. They clattered around, moving two tables together, and made animated conversation.

'Does Jason like him?'

'I think so. They seemed to get on all right, although for Jason I think the main thing was just being in the park with a man. Afterwards Simon asked him all kinds of questions about school. I was impressed; he was really good with him.'

Holly buttered her bread.

'Has he asked about Jason's dad?' Holly asked carefully.

'Yes, I just said I was widowed and I'd prefer not to talk about it and left it at that. He hasn't asked since, which is a relief.'

'Slowly, slowly, Cathy. Take care. It's a tentative and promising start. But you need to be careful with strangers, people are often not what they seem.'

'God, don't I know it,' Cathy muttered under her breath.

'What's that, darling?'

'Nothing.' Cathy looked away. 'Look, I'm not naive.'

'I just don't want to see you and Jason hurt again.' Holly paused and rubbed her chin. 'You know, I respect that you don't want to talk about it, but it would help if you would tell me something at least about what happened to Jason's dad... ' she said softly, 'when and how he passed

24

away... give me some perspective on things.'

Cathy gave Holly a piercing stare and turned away, grimacing. 'Don't go there again, please. You agreed not to talk about him.'

'I know it must be hurting, it can't be easy keeping it all inside. As soon as I mention him you go stiff.'

Cathy sighed heavily.

'Yes, I suppose I do. People are so nosy, and not in a good way.' There was exasperation in her voice.

The waitress put a cafétière, cup and saucer plus jug of milk on the table and there was a pleasant smell of fresh roast coffee. Holly's expression became serious as she poured the coffee, tore open a little white sugar bag and slowly stirred in the sugar.

'I hope you don't think I'm like that. We've been friends so long, although I know I wasn't around when Jason was born. I'm sorry about that.'

'Yes, I missed you. It seemed like you were away for years and years, but I know it was only five.'

'Four.'

'Miss it, California I mean?'

'Yes, sometimes... I miss the warmth, especially on a cold March morning like today.'

'Look, I know you're trying to support me. The only person who I told was my gay friend Lance, who supported me when Jason was a baby.'

'The one who died of AIDS?'

'Yes, I haven't told anyone else, not even my mum, believe it or not, which is probably why I feel so dreadfully alone, and also why she and I are a bit estranged. Please don't be offended, it's not that I don't trust you, it's... my choice, Holly.'

'I know... but I'm not sure how long you can keep this up.'

Cathy looked away and shook her head.

25

'I'm concerned for you,' said Holly.

'Look, Simon's very busy and so are you, but I'll try and arrange for you to meet, OK?'

Holly snatched open her handbag and pulled out her diary.

'Very good idea. I'll see when I'm free.'

CHAPTER 4

Approaching the school, Cathy felt a shiver run down her spine. She stopped for a moment. Dipping her hand into her trouser pocket she pulled out the letter from Mrs Scully, the headmistress, and read it again: '…to discuss with you some important issues concerning Jason's welfare.' The signature in black ink was clear and neat. Grimacing, she folded the letter and put it into her handbag. On reaching the gates she glanced up at the brightly painted notice board for Manor House Infant School, Brandon Wood. She squared her shoulders and took a deep breath.

As the receptionist told her to take a seat, Cathy detected just a hint of contempt in the woman's expression and shivered again. Perched on the edge of the chair she felt a similar kind of trepidation, ridiculous as it was, that she had as a girl when called to see the head teacher. She was transported back in time to that smoking incident behind the bike shed; there was also the truancy from class 9 one bright sunny day when she absconded to the park with two friends, and then there was the netball match incident… She chuckled quietly to herself.

After what seemed an interminable wait, Cathy heard the click-clack of shoes as Miss Andrews, the secretary, crossed the parquet floor. Such an officious woman: maybe she is there simply to intimidate the parents, mused Cathy.

'Mrs Scully will see you now.' Cathy followed her down the school corridor, a bright space with children's pictures and their first attempts at story writing on lined white paper mounted on bright-coloured card and pinned up on the walls. The office was right at the end. 'In here, please.'

Mrs Scully rose from behind her neatly ordered desk. The office was cool and gloomy; overhanging trees outside obscured the view from the window.

'Ah, Mrs Simpson, do come in and sit down.' The tone of her voice demanding attention and obedience, Mrs Scully gestured towards a pair of padded chairs near a bookcase neatly filled with children's books. She pulled out a chair for herself and Cathy sat opposite. Mrs Scully was dressed in a linen skirt with matching jacket and neat court shoes, her hair stiffly set. She smoothed her skirt as she sat down. 'You must be wondering what this is all about,' she said, awkwardly.

'Yes, I am rather. I hope nothing is wrong.'

There was a subtle smell of plasticine. Looking down, Cathy saw cubes of colourful modelling clay in a box along with plastic moulds depicting animals.

'Well, Mrs Simpson, as I said in my letter, I want to discuss Jason with you. He is a very interesting boy, very capable,' she hesitated and frowned, 'but there is some cause for concern.'

'Oh?'

'Let me first of all say he shows excellent ability in Mathematics. He particularly likes playing with his abacus and counting out loud.'

'Yes, I know, he does this at home.'

'Ah, does he? He's good at reading and writing as well, which is most gratifying. His teachers are impressed with his quick grasp of ideas. He has some interest in sport too, I believe.'

'Yes, football. Every chance he gets he's kicking a ball about,' said Cathy, brightly.

'Does he have friends to play football with?' Mrs Scully scrutinised her.

Cathy frowned; it was a blunt question.

'Not many, he's not that sociable, unfortunately. He's a

28

bit of a loner, like...' Cathy paused.

'Like?' prompted Mrs Scully.

'Er, like many kids,' said Cathy, reddening a little.

'So true,' said Mrs Scully with a slight smile. 'Well, that's what I wanted to talk to you about.' She coughed, clearing her throat. 'As we are a small primary school, the teachers take pride in knowing each child individually and we work closely as a team. As headmistress I have overall responsibility and usually do not get involved with individual pupils unless there is a particular need. When I'm alerted to concerns I like to investigate further so that we can deal with problems before they become issues... His class teacher, Miss Arnold, has been particularly concerned.'

Cathy stiffened. 'What is the problem?'

Mrs Scully coughed again.

'You may know Mr Baker, here at the school?'

'Yes, he's the caretaker, isn't he?'

Mrs Scully sniffed. 'He has a number of different roles, but we prefer the term "Sports Officer",' she said sternly.

'Oh.'

'The point is... ' She frowned. 'Jason's been asking Mr Baker to play football with him in the park. If it was a one-off we wouldn't take much notice but this happened more than once last term and now this summer term.'

'Oh, I see. That's odd. I didn't know that.'

'Jason also says,' Mrs Scully twisted her thumbs and frowned again, 'that his Daddy can't take him out at the moment because he's away and won't be coming home for a very long time. When he does come home he's going to play football with him, help him with his abacus and watch television with him.'

Cathy felt her heart start to pound; she twisted the gold band, which she had bought for herself, on her ring finger.

'I see.'

29

'He's also mentioned this several times to different members of staff: Miss Arnold, Mr Baker and also Mrs Crowther, the dinner lady.' Mrs Scully leaned over and patted Cathy's hand. 'I know how difficult it can be for children who have lost a parent, especially at such a young age,' she said quietly, in a protective, motherly way. 'They don't have the maturity to understand or express their grief, although I know Jason's father died when Jason was very young. That is right, isn't it?'

'Jason didn't know his father, never met him,' said Cathy curtly.

'Well, the point is, Mrs Simpson, that we at the school are concerned that Jason needs to come to terms with his father's death, maybe he needs professional help.' She cocked her head to one side and looked intently at Cathy.

Cathy felt her chest swell and her throat tighten.

'This is all a surprise to me. I didn't know Jason was talking like this and I've no idea why,' she said quickly.

'I see.' Mrs Scully frowned. 'He's not like some of our children who live in a fanciful creative world, which makes Jason more of a concern to us.' She twisted her thumbs again. 'He is an intelligent little boy but his sharp mind needs to be tempered with reality.'

Cathy took a deep breath.

'Jason's welfare is my first priority. Thanks for bringing this to my attention.'

Mrs Scully looked intently at her, as if waiting for her to say something else. The atmosphere suddenly felt oppressive and claustrophobic. Cathy promptly stood up. 'Now, if there's nothing else I need to go to work; I'm already late.'

Mrs Scully rose from her chair.

'Yes, I understand your need to work as a widowed mother.' She smiled sympathetically. 'Thank you for coming today, I'm glad we've had this meeting. And please, feel free to make another appointment with me so that we can continue to work together in Jason's best interests.'

'Please be reassured I will deal with this as a matter of urgency, Mrs Scully.'

'I hope so, Mrs Simpson.'

'Good day.'

They shook hands.

Cathy walked briskly down the road. The sun was warm on her face but there was a cool morning breeze. The avenue of trees was adorned with red and pink blossom bursting with life. She walked the short distance to the park and sat on a bench. It felt cold and damp under her trousers. Dog walkers passed by. In the distance she heard toddlers playing in the playground.

Despite her efforts, tears trickled down her cheeks. She leant forwards, her face in her hands. How could I have got it so wrong with Jason, she thought. I've been dithering, maybe giving him mixed messages. He's picked up on my odd comment here and there; I must be more careful. Now he's fantasising, hoping for a Daddy to do fatherly things with him. My poor boy. I can never replace a father, however hard I try. Did I make the wrong decisions all those years ago? How can I know? I did what I thought was right at the time. Oh God, I'm so confused...

As she pondered there was the sweet smell of spring rose blossom; she sat back momentarily and closed her eyes, drawing in the scent. Relaxing, her mind drifted and she remembered the floral dress she wore that fateful summer day in 1980, six years ago. She recalled being in the office of Mr Dunn, the solicitor, on Harrow High Road. She'd never been to Harrow before and had no idea why she had been summoned there. She remembered the faint smell of furniture polish and the leather-covered desk, the silver Parker pen and on the wall a portrait of an austere businessman whose eyes seemed to be staring at her. The room was shadowy and dark. The scene replayed in her mind, as it had dozens of times since.

'Miss Simpson, I expect you're wondering why I've asked you here.' Mr Dunn, seated behind his desk, peered at her through half-moon spectacles. He was a rotund, balding man in a pinstriped suit.

'Yes, I am.'

'You have no idea?'

'No idea whatever.'

He cleared his throat.

'It concerns Blake Carter.'

She took a deep breath. 'Blake Carter?'

'I presume he didn't tell you about the arrangements he's made for you.'

'Arrangements?' She shook her head.

'Provisions. He wanted to secure your future financially, at least in the short term.'

'What do you mean?' She felt a wave of heat overwhelm her.

Mr Dunn put down the pen he had been fiddling with and looked intently at her. 'I've had many dealings with Mr Carter over the years and he has always been very thorough and clear about his plans, although I am rather surprised that, in this instance, he chose to keep this from you. However, he must have had his reasons.'

'What plans, please explain.' She rubbed her stomach, feeling a little nauseous; this was the second time this week.

'Mr Carter came to me, two months ago. He wanted to put his affairs in order before he... well... we discussed the various options; I gave him some advice. A week or so later he returned, having made his decision, and gave me instructions as to how he wanted his assets dealt with.' Mr Dunn got up and walked to the window, looked out briefly, then turned round and faced her. 'One of the things he was most intent upon was your financial security.'

'Mine, my financial security?'

'Yes, he was most insistent upon it.' Mr Dunn looked at her quizzically and took a deep breath. 'He has transferred ownership of his flat into your name.'

'Me? My name?' She felt her heart palpitate wildly.

'Yes, you are now the legal owner of the flat in Conway Place, although because of legal and taxation considerations you will not own the flat outright for another five years. There were complex technicalities which we needed to take account of when transferring the deeds.'

Cathy sat in silence, wide-eyed. She grabbed the wooden arms of her chair, feeling she might fall over and faint.

'You look stunned, Miss Simpson.' He sat down again.

She shook her head. 'I didn't know anything about this... I don't know what to say.'

'I know this must be all rather a shock, especially in the circumstances.' He studied her candidly for a few moments. 'It is a lot to take in.' He cleared his throat. 'It is obviously a rather delicate subject but Mr Carter has left me an address should there be any unresolved issues.'

'He has?' She took a deep breath, to collect herself.

'Yes.'

'I see.'

'I just wanted you to know.'

Cathy nodded, still gripping the arms of the chair to stabilise herself. She sat back and took another deep breath.

He opened a drawer of his desk and withdrew a document.

'I can explain the legal situation now for you if you like, or you can take this document away and read it at

33

your leisure.'

A pigeon came to rest on the windowsill with a clattering of wings; it walked up and down nodding and cooing, then flew away into the distance.

'I'll take the document, thank you.'

He passed it to her.

'I have the keys here for you.' He opened a drawer, pulled out some keys and bounced them in his hand. 'From what I understand, the flat is empty so you can make it your own from today.' He passed them to her. The keys had a large white paper label attached to them with brown string. Cathy read "*Flat 6, Conway Place, Brandon Wood*" in bold handwriting that she didn't recognise. She felt the smoothness of the metal between her fingers.

'You may think that's enough to take in for now, Miss Simpson, but Mr Carter was always very thorough.' He fingered through some papers on his desk. 'He wanted you to have a monthly income to pay for the council rates, ground rent, bills, etc. so he has also made provision for this.'

'He has?' Her jaw dropped.

'He had a significant amount of capital which is tied up in stocks and shares. He's used this to create a trust fund for you. As a result you will be paid a regular monthly income. Of course, stocks and shares fluctuate in value, but he's fixed this amount for five years so whatever the stock market does your income will be regular and dependable. After this, if you wish to instruct me to act as your legal representative in this regard I can do so. Maybe you will need some time to consider this.'

Cathy sat speechless for a while. She put her hand to her stomach. The nausea was rising again.

'You look rather pale, if you don't mind me saying. Would you like a coffee, Miss Simpson?'

'No, but a stiff whisky will do,' she quipped.

'Sorry,' he chuckled. 'We don't keep liquor. This profession demands the utmost sobriety at all times. Our clients would expect nothing less of us.'

'OK then, the coffee... and a glass of water, please.'

He rang a bell.

A smartly dressed and efficient-looking woman walked in.

'A coffee and a glass of water for our visitor, please, Mrs Nolan.'

'Of course, Mr Dunn.'

Cathy tried to pull herself together.

'He's thought of everything... '

'Yes, it's not often I have to deal with financial matters like this, but every now and then there's an unusual case... '

The images in Cathy's mind became cloudy, the voices indistinct. In the distance she could hear a dog barking. Suddenly jolted back into the moment, she heard a dog panting and smelled its hot breath on her hand. On opening her eyes to the bright daylight she saw a black Labrador upon her, sniffing and wagging its tail wildly. Cathy came to.

'Sorry, he's friendly,' said an obviously well-meaning woman with a Scottish accent, smiling broadly. 'Come along, Dougie, and leave the lady alone.'

'It's all right,' said Cathy.

She noticed the woman was staring at her. 'Sorry, I don't want to intrude but, are you all right?'

'Yes, perfectly.'

'If you're sure... '

Cathy looked away, and after hesitating for a moment the woman walked off, staring back at Cathy from time to time. She sat for a few more minutes then got up and walked across the park; now I am really late for work, I must tidy myself up quickly, she thought.

CHAPTER 5

Cathy stood in the doorway watching as Jason counted his wooden blocks out loud. Crouching on the floor, he put them on top of each other in groups of ten, making little piles. OK, this might be a good moment, she thought. I can't procrastinate any longer, I really must be strong. I need to do this. Jason turned and looked at her.

'Look, Mummy, I've got four sets of ten,' he pointed to them in turn, 'that's forty. And look, that's the same number on my abacus.'

Cathy looked carefully at what he was showing her.

'Yes, you're right, very good,' she smiled.

She came and sat beside him on the floor, tucking one leg under the other.

'I'm going to count up to one hundred, one hundred blocks.'

'Good boy!'

She was quiet for a long moment, watching him count.

'There's something we need to discuss,' she said, swallowing hard, 'about your Daddy.'

Jason stopped counting, sat still with one block in his hand and looked questioningly into her eyes.

'My Daddy?'

'Yes.' She drew closer to him and said softly, 'You know Mrs Scully, the head teacher.'

Jason nodded.

'She says you've been talking about your Daddy coming home.' She took a deep breath. 'You know it's very sad, but your Daddy is gone, gone forever. He's not coming back,' she said quietly.

Jason looked deep into her eyes then grabbed Snowy, his favourite teddy bear, and cuddled it close.

'Is my Daddy dead?' he asked, not looking at her.

Cathy gulped; the rawness of the word felt like a sharp wound.

'Yes, darling, he's dead.'

Jason was still looking away.

'Where do people go to when they die?'

Cathy thought for a moment.

'Well,' she said, 'I believe they go back to where they were before they were born, to a cosy place, full of warmth and sunshine and love.'

'Do they have football there and counting blocks?'

'Well, they might, no one really knows, but I believe it's a place where everyone is happy,' she said slowly and delicately, blinking back tears.

Jason silently rocked Snowy back and forth in his arms for a few moments.

'Not coming back? Not going to play football with me?'

'No... I'm sorry.' She swallowed hard.

Jason looked down and fiddled with a block in his hand. 'I want him to, Mummy, I want to have my Daddy.'

Cathy felt a sharp lump in her throat, and for a moment it was as if she couldn't breathe.

He looked up at her, sadness etched on his face.

'I know. I wish he could be here for you, but he can't be.'

Jason picked up a few more blocks and stacked them one on top of the other, making a tall tower.

'You know, Mummy might meet someone one day and you'll have a new Daddy. Would you like that?'

'Will he play football with me, like that man in the park, the one who gave me my football?'

'I very much hope so, no reason why not.'

Jason turned to her and climbed on her lap. She cuddled him close.

'I love you, Mummy,' he said, looking at her, his eyes full of sadness.

Cathy stifled a sob; she'd rehearsed their conversation so many times, but this had been so much harder than she had imagined. She felt as though her heart would burst.

'And I love you, my darling, always.'

CHAPTER 6

'There's a space,' said Simon, pointing, 'between the red car and the dark blue one.'

Cathy slotted the car neatly into the gap, pulled up the handbrake and switched off the engine. 'Well, here we are,' she said. They got out; Cathy drew in her breath. 'Mmm…' she said, 'smells lovely and fresh. I love it here. It's so easy to get to from my flat, only half an hour by car.'

He looked at his watch. 'Fifteen minutes to twelve, is Holly here already, do you think?'

'She's usually very prompt. Another few minutes and she'll be here I'm sure.'

'Have you known her long?'

'Almost all my life, we were at school together, primary and secondary.'

'That is a long time. I've lost track of all my old school chums.'

'Holly's the only one I see from those days; she's my oldest, and best, friend. We've lived near to each other most of the time, except when we went away to university and then she lived in California for a few years, around the time I had Jason.'

'What was she doing in America?'

'After she did her MSc in London, she got a job with a PR company; they promoted her very quickly and sent her to their Los Angeles office to get international experience.'

'That's impressive. She sounds intimidating.'

'Nonsense, she's really very charming, as you'll find out soon. Come on, I'll show you the lock.' Cathy strode briskly across the car park to the side of the canal, with Simon close behind. At the entrance to the path was a large signpost, 'Grand Union Canal', and underneath a small map of the waterway and towpaths. The water gently trickled between the lock gates, the grassy verges were green and lush. The sun wafted in and out behind fluffy white clouds. Behind the canal mature oak and beech trees extended into dense woods. There was a small white-painted cottage situated on the other side of the canal. Its window boxes were full to bursting with geraniums in full bloom: red, yellow and orange. There was a wooden door, painted green, and beside it was a pair of ceramic wellington boots, with a profusion of blue cornflowers sticking out of the tops.

'Very nice-looking cottage,' said Simon.

'That's the lock-keeper's house,' said Cathy. 'Look, there's a plaque on the wall above the door.'

'Springbridge Lock, 1878,' read Simon. 'That's old.'

'Yes.'

'I wonder if the lock-keeper lives here all year round.'

'Yes, he does.'

'Must get a bit lonely here in the depths of winter, when there's no one going up and down the canal.'

'I suppose it must, although I expect only self-reliant types would take on the job. There must be quite a few of them, there being quite a lot of locks on the canal. But not every lock has a lock-keeper.'

'Oh, so who operates the lock when there's no one there?' asked Simon.

'People on the boats going through.'

'I see, they must be easy to operate then.'

'I think so. You soon get the hang of it.'

In front of the cottage two canal boats were moored, the skippers waiting their turn to enter the lock.

'Have you seen a lock before, Simon?'

'No, can't say I have. Not that I remember anyway.'

'Well, you see those big wooden gates in front of the first narrow boat?' Simon looked where Cathy was pointing. A pair of wooden gates, firmly shut, towered above the lead canal boat. 'And the second pair of gates…' She pointed further up.

'No need to explain. I know about this sort of thing.'

The gate in front of the canal boat swung open slowly. When it was fully open the skipper on the lead boat steered it through the gap and moored in front of a second set of wooden gates. Simon and Cathy walked along the towpath to the next gates. The second boat came through the open gate and was moored behind the first one. Once it was safely through, the gate swung shut again. Directly in front of the gate the water was churning, small whirlpools forming and collapsing as the water rushed in.

'Comes in fast, doesn't it,' Simon remarked.

'Yes, it doesn't take long to fill. Or to empty, going the other way.' Cathy turned and scanned the car park. 'Here's Holly now,' she said. 'That bright red car just parking up.'

'Nice motor.'

'Yes, it's a company car. I'm going back to my car to change into my boots,' Cathy said. 'Let's go and say hello to Holly.'

They reached Holly's car just as she was closing the boot. 'Hi,' she said. She was dressed in khaki trousers, trekking boots and light raincoat.

Cathy gave her a hug. 'This is Simon,' she said, smiling eagerly.

Holly and Simon shook hands. 'I'm very pleased to meet you,' said Holly, scrutinising him quickly and feeling the slightly damp hand in hers.

'And I'm pleased to meet you,' said Simon.

'Are you all set?' asked Holly.

'Not quite, I'm just going to put my boots on,' said Cathy. 'Back in a minute.' She trotted off.

'What about you, Simon. Are you changing?' said Holly, eyeing his suede shoes.

41

'What?' He looked down at his feet. 'I don't own any boots.'

'No boots?' Holly raised one eyebrow. 'Not even an old pair of shoes you don't mind getting scuffed?'

'No. I have got a pair of football boots now; I got them so I could play football with Jason. But other than that, nothing. I wasn't expecting to be hiking.'

'It's been raining quite heavily the last few days, I hope your shoes don't get ruined.'

'Me too. What's the path like?'

'Mostly stony, but it does become a dirt track further up.'

Holly detected a slight frown on Simon's face.

Cathy rejoined them. 'Ready,' she said.

'Cathy, Simon was just telling me he bought football boots so he could play with Jason. That's nice. Jason must be pleased about that.'

'He is,' said Cathy. 'You've been out in the park with Jason twice now, isn't it?'

'Yes, twice.'

'Jason loves it, he comes home so happy. Simon's so caring.' Cathy gave him a little kiss on the lips.

'Great little boy, your Jason.' Simon hugged Cathy close and looked into her eyes.

Holly gave them a moment. 'Well, when you're ready, I'm ready,' she said.

The towpath was not wide enough to walk all abreast so Cathy took the lead.

'You two get to know each other,' she said.

Holly and Simon walked together. To their left was a straggly hedge of hawthorn bushes, interspersed with clumps of brambles. Behind the hedge was a long line of trees parallel to the canal, their branches overhanging the path. As the trio walked along, beside them on their right the dark brown water flowed sluggishly past.

'Where are you from, Simon?' asked Holly. 'Where's your home town?'

'I live in Watford at the moment. I was born in Coventry, but I haven't been there for years and years. My family moved around quite a bit while I was growing up, except when I was at prep school, and my work has meant I haven't stayed in any one place very long either.'

'Cathy tells me you're a salesman, selling industrial air-conditioning units.'

Simon darted a glance at Cathy, who was now a considerable distance in front of them. 'That's not accurate,' he said tightly.

'Sorry, have I got that wrong?'

'It's not just a matter of sales; I also do a business appraisal and costing. We like to make sure the product we're promoting suits the business infrastructure.'

'Oh, what does that involve?'

'I visit a potential client's site and make recommendations on what they'll need based on their ongoing business development strategy.'

Travelling salesman, thought Holly. 'I see,' she said. 'Do you enjoy it? It must be quite demanding, I imagine.'

'It does involve long hours, and often I have to travel to clients' sites in other parts of the country, but it's very satisfying when we get the orders as a result.'

'What's the name of your company?'

'Venture Cooling Systems.'

'I can't say I've heard of them.'

'We were only established five years ago but the business has grown rapidly. Another ten years and it'll be a well-recognised brand name, I'm sure.' Simon smiled confidently. 'You're in management as well, very good at your job, Cathy tells me. A chain of fashion shops, isn't it?'

'Yes, I manage the shops for "Ladies In Vogue". I hope you've heard of them, otherwise I may need to have words

43

with our PR department.'

'I have, in fact. Believe it or not I go to your associated company "Men In Vogue" for some of my clothes.'

'That's very good to hear. That's the top end of the market we cater for, of course, designer labels almost exclusively. By the way, how are your shoes holding up?'

Simon looked at his feet.

'Not too bad, considering.'

'I'm glad. I wouldn't want you to ruin them.' As the path narrowed Holly took the lead and they finished talking. They walked for another quarter of a mile. Further up, Holly stopped. 'Oh look, that's so cute,' she said. 'That little dog on the boat.' She pointed.

Simon looked at the water and saw an old rusting canal boat chugging along with a grizzled man at the rear operating the tiller. A large black and white dog with floppy ears sat upright at his feet.

'Funny,' said Simon, 'I didn't think people would have a dog on a canal boat.'

'Oh yes,' said Holly. 'I've noticed lots of dogs on boats.'

There was a smell of diesel as fumes spewed out from the exhaust. They came to a small brick bridge that spanned the canal. Cathy stood on the middle, watching the ducks floating by. Holly and Simon walked up and joined her.

'What do you think?' asked Cathy. 'Do you reckon we've walked far enough?'

'Well, Simon?' asked Holly.

'I think that's enough, it's looking muddier up ahead,' said Simon. 'That pub the other side of the car park, *The Swan*, looked inviting. Is that where you're planning we have lunch?'

'Yes, their food is good,' said Cathy. 'But we mustn't be too long because I need to be home before Jason comes back from school.'

'Then let's go,' said Holly.

They trooped down to the towpath and turned to walk back the way they had come. The boat with the man and dog moored up in the distance in front of them. As they approached, the dog jumped into the canal and swam a few yards before clambering out nearby and trotting up to them.

'Oh look,' said Cathy. 'He's come to say hello. Isn't that sweet.'

The dog stopped in front of Simon and shook itself vigorously, scattering water droplets everywhere, drenching Simon's clothes, then lazily trotted off. Suddenly Simon's posture and demeanour changed, his face flushed red, he bared his teeth.

'Fucking dog,' he shouted furiously.

'Oh dear,' said Cathy, putting her hand to her mouth.

'I'd prefer not to be sprayed with dirty canal water,' he snarled, and pulling out a handkerchief from his pocket he wiped himself down. 'Just look at my clothes.' Holly and Cathy exchanged glances. Simon mumbled more expletives under his breath, but after a few moments his tone softened and he smiled at them both. 'But I don't want to let that spoil spending time with you two, especially my darling Cathy. Let's forget all about this.'

'They can be washed,' Cathy said, hesitantly.

'Of course,' he said, beaming a smile, and gently reached for her hand.

CHAPTER 7

'Hello, is that you, Simon?' Cathy shouted from the kitchen.

She was expecting him and had left the door ajar.

'Yes, I've brought someone to meet you,' he shouted back.

Cathy emerged from the kitchen and looked down the corridor. Next to Simon stood a smartly dressed woman of mature years with set dark brown hair.

'Cathy, this is my mother, Margaret. Mother, this is Cathy.'

'Oh,' said Cathy, 'I... I... thought we'd agreed I'd meet your mother at *The Rose and Crown* for lunch sometime.'

'You don't mind, do you?' Simon took off his coat and hung it up.

'No, of course not, you're most welcome. It's... just unexpected, that's all.'

'My goodness, we wouldn't want to put you out, my dear.' Margaret's voice was clipped and cultured.

'No, it's fine,' said Cathy. 'I was just doing the washing. I'll finish up if you don't mind. Please,' she gestured towards the living room, 'make yourselves at home.'

Cathy went back into the kitchen.

Alone with Simon in the hallway, Margaret scanned the long corridor in front of her and the layout of the flat. On her way towards the living room she peered through the wide open door into Jason's bedroom.

'What a sweet room.' She stepped in and looked around.

Simon gestured, 'This way, Mother.'

'Oh yes.'

Margaret followed him into the living room.

'Good size.' She walked to the window. Across the busy street was a park with a pond and playground in the distance. 'An excellent position.'

Flustered, Cathy came in, thrusting her hands into her pockets. 'I'm sorry for the delay.'

Margaret settled herself on the sofa.

'No matter, my dear, all busy mothers need to do chores.'

'Er, yes... can I get you some tea or coffee?'

'No, do come and sit next to me, Cathy.' She patted the sofa. 'I want to hear all about you.'

Cathy did as she was asked and perched next to her. Simon sat in the armchair opposite, watching. She smelled Margaret's subtle, sweet perfume.

'Simon has told me so much about you. I have been so looking forward to meeting you.'

'Oh, thank you.'

'This flat seems very nice. And I can see there's a playground across the road. Do you take Jason there?'

Cathy looked towards the window.

'Yes, I do, when I can.'

'And I believe you work?'

'Yes, part-time.'

'In a solicitor's office.'

'Yes.'

Margaret reached for Cathy's hand and held it. Cathy submitted passively but sat back slightly. Margaret's hand was small and cool.

'Are you sure you wouldn't like some tea?' Cathy asked.

'No, my dear, I would much rather talk to you.'

'I'll make the teas,' said Simon, sitting forward, 'so you can get to know each other.'

'Oh, OK,' said Cathy. Gently she withdrew her hand and waited.

Simon got up and went to the kitchen.

'And how do you find it, working?'

'It's fine. It fits in around Jason's school.'

'What school does he go to? Is it nearby?'

'Yes, we can walk. It's only a few roads away. Manor House Infants.'

'Are you happy with the school?'

'Yes, it's good, Jason seems happy.'

'That's so important, isn't it... Is he here now, can I meet him? I hear he is such a dear little boy.'

'No, he's with a school friend.'

'Another time then.'

'Er... yes.'

There was an awkward silence for a few moments.

'What do you like doing, for yourself?'

Cathy shrugged and looked at the ceiling.

'Well, I'm quite busy; I don't have a lot of time to myself.'

Margaret patted Cathy's hand.

'Any hobbies?'

Cathy thought for a moment.

'Well, before I had Jason I used to enjoy rock climbing.'

'How interesting, where did you go to do this climbing?'

'The Peak District mainly, but I haven't been able to go for years now.'

'Shame, because of Jason?'

'Yes, he's too young for me to take him with me at the moment.'

'So you're not able to get away by yourself?'

'No, I wouldn't leave Jason.'

'You can leave Jason with Simon and myself; when he comes back in I'll ask him.'

'Oh, OK... that would be... helpful.'

'No trouble at all, my dear, anything to help.' Margaret looked round, considering. 'What else do you enjoy doing?'

Cathy thought for a few moments. 'I like visiting museums and reading *New Scientist*. I like to keep up with developments in technology.'

'You have a science background Simon tells me?'

'Yes, I have a combined degree in Chemistry and Biology.'

'How clever. Simon is very good at electronics. He might have told you this already, but when he was at work placement during his sixth form he impressed the manager so much that they offered him a job straight away.'

'Yes, he told me.'

'And did he tell you how much his starting salary was?'

'I don't recall... '

'It was the same as they offered new graduates. They wanted him that much!'

'Well... yes... '

'So I'm sure two scientific minds are very compatible.'

They sat in silence for a few moments. Cathy played with her fingers. She's quite inquisitive, overwhelming almost, but in a good way, thought Cathy. I suppose I should even the balance, show some interest in her.

'So, tell me about yourself.' Cathy coughed, clearing her throat.

'Oh, nothing to tell, nothing of significance anyway.'

'What do you like doing?'

'Just the normal things ladies of my age do. There are all my societies and my card evenings, and I have a huge network of acquaintances; it keeps me very busy.' Simon returned with a tray full of teas and handed out cups. Margaret looked up at Simon. 'We'll look after Jason so Cathy can go rock climbing, won't we, Simon?'

'Of course, we'd be really happy to. We'll arrange this

for July or August, shall we? I know Cathy prefers fair weather.'

'Well, I have done it all year round but summer is best. Thank you, I'll... I'll give it some thought... the planning.'

There was a break in conversation while they sipped their tea.

'Did you ever work yourself, employment I mean?' asked Cathy.

'I remember you working in that accounts office,' said Simon.

'Oh yes, I did, I like to keep busy, but it was not for the money of course, only for the interest.' She looked inquiringly at Cathy. 'Now, do you like to cook?' She patted Cathy on the knee.

'I'm not much good, I'm afraid.'

'Simon tells me you make an excellent casserole.'

'It's about the only thing I can cook,' Cathy chuckled.

'Do you have a big kitchen here?'

'It's just standard size, I think.'

'Sometimes it makes a difference if the kitchen is laid out well and there's sufficient storage; it encourages you to cook.'

'Oh.'

'What about your larder, dear, is it a decent size? The more dried ingredients you can store the better I find. You can put your hand on whatever you want when you need it. I'm quite partial to herbs and spices so I have a lot, two shelves full of them.'

'Well, I'd say the space is adequate.' She looked over at Simon. 'You can see it for yourself if you like.'

'Well... only if it's no trouble.'

'No, not at all.'

They all went into the kitchen and Margaret looked around.

'Yes, it's all perfectly adequate in here, and a nice big

floor space, I'd say bigger than average.'

'When Jason was a toddler he played in here all the time when I was doing chores.'

'Perfect, perfect.'

'Cathy spends a lot of time in here,' said Simon. 'The other rooms, they're quite big as well, and don't get much use really, do they, darling?'

'Are they?' Margaret's eyes widened.

'Yes,' said Simon.

'It is quite a big flat,' said Cathy.

'Oh, I'd be interested to see the other rooms sometime, but I don't want to bother you, not now.'

Strange she's so interested, but there's no harm in showing her, thought Cathy.

'No, please, I'd be happy to show you,' she said. Margaret looked around carefully, peering into corners and out of the windows, commenting on the generous space and the attractive views as she went. Afterwards they hovered in the hallway.

'What a lovely space you have here.' She took Cathy's hand again. 'Some single parents live in such confined spaces but you can spread yourself out nicely here, can't you?' She put her finger on her mouth, deliberating. 'I have a big house. That's why Simon and I don't get on top of each other. When he said he wanted to stay for a while I didn't even need to hesitate, but maybe it's a bit big for me now.'

'You've been saying that for years, Mother.'

'Maybe I have… but perhaps a flat is what I need.'

Simon put his hands in his pockets and jingled his car keys.

'I think I'd better take you home before it gets late. You've got your bridge evening later, haven't you?'

'Yes, well... ' Margaret took Cathy's hand. 'How lovely to meet you, Cathy, I'll look forward to seeing you again very soon and meeting little Jason.'

Cathy saw them to the door.

'Well, goodbye,' she said. She watched them go down the stairs. She's a strange woman, Cathy thought. But nice, all the same.

* * *

Margaret settled down beside Simon and fastened her seat belt. There was a fresh smell of lavender wafting from the air-freshener on the dashboard. Simon pulled out on to the open road.

'So, what do you think of her?'

'Well, she's a bit of an enigma, isn't she?'

The sun poured through the window. Margaret put on her sunglasses.

'Why do you say that?'

'Well, she's a plain, ordinary little thing. She doesn't make the most of herself at all, that short boyish haircut, slacks and T-shirt. I wouldn't say she's sloppy exactly, just un-groomed. I'd like to see her with some make-up and she needs to grow her hair and visit a stylist. All the same, she has a well-proportioned, trim figure. If she was my daughter I'd take her to a quality boutique and make her try on some chic clothes; a dress would suit her I think. Then she could, potentially, be quite attractive.'

'I think she is attractive, actually. I take your point about her needing make-up though.'

'Yes, buy her some, get her to wear it.'

'What's with her being an enigma?'

'Well, she's obviously quite intelligent, in an academic sort of way, but I'm not sure how astute she is. She must be on a lowish income. Are you sure she owns the flat?'

'Yes, I am.'

'Well, in that case, how did she come by it?'

'I've tried to get it out of her but she won't tell me.'

'Why not, what is she hiding?'

'I don't know. I've been through her papers; she has this filing cabinet where she keeps all her official documents and bills. When she was out collecting Jason one afternoon I went through them.'

'That was resourceful of you.'

'I take after you, Mother.' He glanced at her and winked.

'What did you find out?'

'Well, it's quite interesting. The deeds of the flat are in her name, but there was some legal jargon I didn't understand, something about some sort of deed of variation.'

'Go on.'

'Just a minute.'

Simon changed lanes and manoeuvred round two roundabouts.

'There's a lot of traffic here for this time of day.' Margaret wound down the window. 'I'm feeling hot. It's ridiculously warm for May.' Simon wound down his window and a warm breeze wafted in. Margaret peeled off her jacket from under her seat belt. Simon glanced over at her.

'Mother, you're not still wearing that old blouse?'

'Nobody can see it under this jacket and I never take the jacket off in public.'

'You could buy new.'

Margaret frowned at him. 'Money is tight, you know that. Anyway, go on.'

'It seems she only owned a certain percentage of it, which increased each year until last year when she owned it outright.'

'How strange. Did she inherit it?'

'I'm not sure. There was someone else's name on the

document but it was scribbled out. She'd pushed so hard she's nearly made a hole in the paper. I couldn't make it out at all, even holding it up to the light.'

'That is odd. I found the flat quite odd as well. It's surprisingly empty, don't you think so? Her son's room is prettily decorated but the rest of the flat, well... it's blank and there's hardly any furniture, as if she doesn't want to stamp her identity on it.'

'I hadn't thought about that but, yes, I suppose so, now you mention it.'

'Anyway, if she does own it outright it must be worth quite a lot of money. It's an enormous flat, bigger than some houses, and in a desirable location. What do you think it's worth?'

'I've been into the local estate agents for a comparison. As an educated guess I'd say £60,000.'

'That's what I'd say. You could definitely buy a three- or four-bedroomed house in Brandon Wood or Pinner for about £55,000. You'd be able to have your workshop in the garden for sure. Even if you bought a house without one with a large enough garden you'd have some money left over to build one.'

'Just my thinking.'

'But how malleable is she? You'd have to convince her, make yourself indispensable. How could you do it?'

'Her son Jason. She said early on that he was her priority so I've been cultivating him. I've been taking him to football.'

'Football. I remember when you went to watch matches with Uncle Sam and Terry. You were very young. You supported... Chelsea, didn't you?'

'Yes.'

'But you weren't *that* keen on football, were you. You're just not sporty.'

'No, but needs must, and as long as I keep her boy

happy she'll be happy. This was the opening I saw. They have this activity at his school called 'Dad's and Sons' Football' and she was unhappy he was left out. I went straight in there and now Jason is my number one fan.'

'Good.'

Simon pulled up at the side of a suburban road in Watford and parked.

Margaret looked out of the window at the neglected Victorian house set back behind mature trees.

'I really must sell this before it costs me any more money.' She sighed. 'The rising damp, the gutters, the roof. It really is throwing good money after bad. The longer I leave it the worse it gets and the less the house is worth. It's a shame I can't afford to set you up on your own when I move.' She sighed. 'A two-bedroom flat should be sufficient for my needs.'

'It's not your fault, Mother. You bailed me out when I needed it and I'm grateful.'

'And what about her? Will she make a good companion for you? You don't want anyone too demanding, do you? I know you; you like to get your own way.'

'I think I can make things work for me.'

'Use your charm, it usually works wonders. She's a nice enough girl and her circumstances make her vulnerable. But you need to keep on top of the situation; don't let things slip.'

'I think I can make this work, Mother, I really do.'

'I hope so; we don't want a disaster like last time, do we?'

'No, I'm shrewder now, don't worry about that.'

CHAPTER 8

Cathy settled down on a grassy knoll overlooking an overgrown path by the side of the canal. Dappled morning sunlight filtering through the trees made a patchwork of sunny areas around her. The air was warm and still and the water flat, like a mirror. The vegetation clinging to the canal's edge and the blue sky with wispy clouds were reflected back in the sluggish bronze water. She trained her eye on a single piece of flotsam and watched it slowly disappear into the distance, carried on gentle currents. On the other side of the canal blackberry bushes and climbing vines were flanked by a row of tall chestnut trees; behind them cows were grazing in the field.

The path had petered out some yards back; she'd walked along just far enough to be out of sight of passers-by and, hopefully, left in peace.

Dipping into her rucksack, she carefully lifted out a box of matches and a bundle of letters tied together with a red bow. Some letters had been in that state of suspension now for five years, since Jason was born. She hadn't forgotten about them, she just didn't know what to do with them. Now there was a new optimism about her; a change was coming, a good change. She needed to fully embrace the future, and that meant moving on. She slipped off the bow and, using finger and thumb, counted them. The letters felt quite alive in her hand, hot and potent with the raw emotion with which she'd written them. Each one was precious and had been penned with an open and full heart to the person she trusted most in the whole world. She'd stopped writing two years ago; that was when she had decided it was too late, she would never send them, although 'never' felt just too final.

She fingered through the envelopes, one by one. It's over, come on, I don't need to read them, there's no point... but maybe... I'll have one last look, remember what it was like... that time, that feeling. One envelope she recognised as important but couldn't remember why. She turned it over and over and hesitated for a moment. OK, yes I will. She pushed her index finger under the flap, breaking the seal, and pulled out the letter handwritten in blue ink.

"10th May 1981

My dearest Blake,

I am so full of happiness and joy I can hardly believe it. I'm wondering if you can as well. What is it? you are thinking. I just want to shout it to you. Well, we have a son! A wonderful, bouncing, healthy baby boy, 7Ibs 10 oz! Born on 2nd April, 3.23am. I've called him Jason. I hope you like that name. I'll just give you a moment to take this in. Yes, read it again, it's true!

When you left I didn't know I was pregnant, I promise! You may remember that sometimes I missed my periods, well I didn't realise I was expecting until four months into the pregnancy. It was all such a shock. At first I couldn't believe it. Most, well not all, of the nurses, midwives and health visitors were kind, and none of them openly condemned me for being on my own, but the wonderful thing is, I wasn't on my own.

Do you remember me telling you about my gay friend Lance? My friend from Exeter? He got in touch when I was about six months pregnant; he'd just got back from America and was looking for somewhere to stay temporarily. We met up a few times and eventually I told him about us. He is, in fact, the only person on the planet I have told the truth to. I trust him completely. I just had to tell someone and I'm so pleased it was him. He was the right person at the right time. He told me about his own secret as well. He was so ashamed and it is so sad. He's been diagnosed with an illness called lymphadenopathy, which is suddenly becoming prevalent in the gay community. It seems to be a rather serious illness and I am quite worried about him. Despite this, Lance has been fantastic. He rents a room a few streets away and works part-time in an estate agent's. He's been there when I've been nauseous, needed someone to talk to or simply company. After Jason was born he rocked him to sleep I can't remember how many times and ran errands for me, buying groceries and nappies. What a hero!"

A bee buzzed round her head; she flicked it with her hand and it flew off. She continued reading.

"Sadly, over the months I've seen him go downhill quite fast, which makes me worried for him. He gets tired and is on heaps of medication. He says helping me and Jason has been wonderful therapy for him.

I've also had my mother here. She came over from Canada two weeks before my due date (Jason was four days late) and was there at the birth. I have to say she has been helpful but I just couldn't bring myself to tell her about you. She has in the past been critical of my choices, probing and challenging. You may remember me telling you. She accepts that I can't tell her but I think she finds it painful. She left about ten days after Jason was born because she had to get back for Bradley, her second husband. You may remember I told you that he has Parkinson's – now he's in a wheelchair. It seems that he relies on my mum almost entirely, for everything... "

Cathy took a deep breath, folded the letter along the original creases and put it back in the envelope. Closing her eyes, she held it to her heart for a few moments then put it carefully on the ground. Out of the corner of her eye she saw a dark green and shiny creature slither under a large rock. Carefully she removed the stone; there lying in the undergrowth was a small grass snake, a yellow collar behind his head. She looked at it, absorbed in its beauty for a few brief moments. It reminded her of the pet corn snake she had had as a child. She felt nostalgic and reached out to touch it, but just at that moment it slithered away. Sighing, she looked back at the bundle of letters, picked up another envelope at random and slit it open with her finger.

"19th November 1981

My dearest Blake,

Our dear little Jason is seven months old and just starting to crawl. I chase him everywhere! But he is such a lively, happy little boy and smiles at me so much. He has a crop of brown curls the same colour as yours and sometimes I swear he has your expressions, although I think I must be imagining it. I enclose a photo of him on his play-mat. Doesn't he look cute!"

She slid the photo from the letter and studied it. The joy mixed with the pain of loss welled up. She swallowed hard. The bright sun in a clear June sky now burned down on her. She slipped the photo back in the envelope and the letters back into the rucksack and found a secluded spot in the shadow of a large oak tree. She cleared an area of bare earth, collected some twigs and built them into a small mound. A robin hopped nearby, cautiously. She watched it as it hopped in and out of the bushes. She put dry moss as kindling in the middle of the twigs, took a match out of the box and struck it. There was no wind at all. The yellow flame licked and the white smoke wafted upwards. As the fire snapped and popped she could taste the smoke at the back of her throat. Sitting cross-legged, she dipped into her rucksack and picked out another letter.

"16th January 1982

My dearest Blake,

How can I tell you this, I am so sad! Don't worry, it's not Jason, he is a fine healthy boy. It is someone else.

My heart is almost broken. After a long, slow and painful decline my dearest friend Lance died yesterday morning. It was one of the saddest days of my life, second only to you leaving. I'd seen him the day before in the hospice and he looked almost like a skeleton, pale skin stretched over bone. It was so, so difficult to see, I really thought I might break down. I kept myself together, but only just. I had to, for his sake. Every moment, I felt I might just burst out crying. He was barely conscious; I don't know if he knew I was there. There were friends from his gay community coming and going all day. They obviously loved him too and I could tell some of them were concerned about their own health. There was lots of hugging going on; we all needed it. He was so young, it seems so cruel. I will miss him so much, true friends are rare. Selfishly, I now wonder who else I can trust... "

Cathy caught her breath, tears gushed from her eyes, her emotions raw as if it were yesterday, or even today. 'That's enough,' she said aloud. She took the first envelope, felt it between her fingers, turned it over and studied it. The only writing on it was his name in her handwriting: 'Blake' in blue ink. She felt the fire warm on her face and bare arms; she smelt the ash in her nostrils and heard the fire crackle. She gently placed the letter over the flame and watched as the corners curled and went grey then black and the paper was consumed by the heat and smouldered into ashes. 'Goodbye, my love,' she said out loud. 'I must move on, I have to move on... Jason and I have to move on.' She placed another letter on the fire. 'You live in him and he is the future.' As the paper smouldered she felt a tear trickle down her cheek. 'I must put him first... I will put him first... I am putting him first.' The tears welled up, cascaded down her cheeks and she sobbed. Letting it all go, it was uninhibited, raw and cathartic. One by one, slowly, because each one mattered, she placed them in the fire. Lastly she threw in the red ribbon and watched as it was consumed by nature's elemental power. She waited and watched without moving and in silence for a long time until the fire subsided and the smoke had stopped billowing. Gingerly she put her finger into the fire, testing the temperature. The ash was warm but didn't burn her. There was a large flat stone nearby. She picked it up and used it to scoop up the remains into her cupped hands. Carefully she stood up, walked to the canal's edge and scattered the ashes into the canal. That was the right thing to do, she said to herself. Afterwards her hands felt dry and raw and she washed them in the cool water.

In contemplative mood now the ritual was over, she felt that that part of her life had finally ended. She stood still for a long time and watched the ashes float away into the distance.

'Now I'm free,' she shouted, flinging her arms wide in the air... or I will be once I've got rid of that damned blue coat. That's the next job for today, a visit to the Oxfam charity shop, she thought.

CHAPTER 9

As Holly approached, Cathy looked up and closed her book.

'I'm sorry it's taken me so long to meet up. It's work, of course, I've hardly stopped for breath.' Holly sat herself down opposite Cathy at the table in the garden centre café and let out a sigh.

'Good busy, I hope.'

'Business is doing fine, despite the recession. There have been endless problems the last couple of months getting the summer stock on the shop floor. We're using a new supplier, a more sophisticated range. Also, I've got more shops to look after.'

'Anyway, you're here now, and I'm pleased to see you.'

'I will always find time for you.'

Cathy smiled at her friend. 'Thanks, Holly, that's nice.'

'How are you? You look well.'

'I'm good, and so is Jason.'

'Excellent.'

'Can I get you a coffee?' asked Cathy.

'No need, I ordered on the way in, they're bringing it.'

'Anyway, what did you think of him? You liked him, didn't you? You seemed to be getting on well,' said Cathy and took a sip at her cappuccino.

Holly clicked her handbag shut and placed it on the chair beside her. She sat back, crossed her arms and looked at Cathy.

'Do you need my endorsement?'

'No, but I value your opinion.' Cathy smiled enthusiastically. 'You seemed to enjoy chatting to him in the pub about telesales and following leads.'

'Yes, workwise we have a lot in common. He certainly

seems motivated, single-minded and persistent. I expect he's good at his job.'

'Like you that way then.'

Holly drew in her breath.

'Well, I'll be candid. He's a good communicator, he was, not charming exactly, but easy to communicate with most of the time, but, to be honest, I did find him a bit uptight about certain things.'

'Like?'

'Hmm... Let me think now... ' She looked up at the ceiling, remembering, then back again at Cathy. 'He was explaining his calendar with his appointments to me. He didn't say so exactly but I picked up that he seems very put out when his clients cancel or delay, and to be honest, I thought he was over-reacting. This is just part of the job I expect. It seemed to me he doesn't cope well with change and is a bit inflexible. He wants everything wrapped up just as he likes it.'

'Well, that's not much; we're all like that sometimes, aren't we?'

The waitress bought Holly the cafétière, jug of milk and cup on a tray. Holly smiled at her. 'Thank you.' There was a smell of fresh-ground coffee.

'But there is one thing that bothered me.'

'Oh, what's that?'

Holly cleared her throat and poured the coffee into the cup.

'I did think his mood changed quickly when that dog splattered him with water. He was really put out.'

Cathy grimaced. 'Yes, but he recovered quickly, didn't he?'

'Yes, that's true, he did.' Holly glanced at her briefly, leant forward, stirred some sugar into her coffee and looked around. 'We must come to this garden centre more often, I feel like I'm in a country cottage with all these checked tablecloths and the ribbon tiebacks on the curtains.'

'Yes, I like it here.'

'Lucky it's so empty today. This table is in a perfect position right here in the corner – we have a good view of the whole place. There's a danger I might sit here all day.'

'You said on the phone you only had an hour.'

'Yes, that's right.' Holly looked at her watch and slowly sipped her coffee. 'So, back to Simon. He enjoys his work but he seemed to me to be unsettled.'

'He wants to start up his own business eventually. He doesn't want to work with or for anyone else after his bad experiences.'

'Well, if he does, that could be quite disruptive and stressful. Starting a business can be full on. You know it can take years to become established.'

'At the start maybe. I have confidence he'll be successful. If he worked from his mother's house, in the short term at least, we'd see a lot more of him and he's dying to get off the road.'

'Yes, he said he's not happy with all the travelling,' said Holly.

'He gets so tired,' said Cathy.

A silver-haired couple carrying a teapot and cakes on a tray took an adjacent table.

'Hmm... ' Holly looked out of the window for a moment. 'Well, the main thing is, Cathy, does he make you happy? He was very attentive to you.'

'He does, Holly.' She frowned. 'He's not perfect exactly, maybe he's a little obsessed with his appearance, but the other things make up for it.'

'What things, exactly?'

'He's so good with Jason. He really is quite a changed boy since Simon came along. It's a transformation.' Cathy sat forward. 'You know I was called in to see the

64

headmistress.'

'No, I didn't know; why was that?'

'Nothing much really, just they were concerned about Jason's emotional development, probably over-reacting. But you know, over the last six weeks or so he's been so different. He's more communicative, he's sleeping better, more affectionate. Simon gives him so much attention. His class teacher told me only yesterday she's noticed a difference in him. That's huge, Holly, huge.'

'Yes, that is very important.'

'It's the most important thing. What I want really comes second. When Jason is happy, I'm happy. So what makes Jason happy makes me happy. It's as simple as that.'

'He's breaking up for the summer soon, isn't he?'

'There's a couple of weeks to go yet'

'He'll go to the holiday club as usual?'

'Yes, the one in Brandon Wood community hall, he's quite happy and settled there. I send him there on my days off sometimes, I think it does him good to mix with other children. He can be quite a loner.'

'Sounds like a good idea.'

'I think so.'

'I have to admit, you do seem to have blossomed a little. But you must think of your own needs as well.'

'He's very caring and patient towards me. You know... it's been a long time since I've been, well, intimate... as you know,' she whispered.

'Yes, I do know.'

'And... because of Jason we've only managed it a few times... but I'm pleased to report he's a good lover, he's slow and sensitive. Again, it's not earth-shattering exactly, but it's so good to be loved, and I feel like a woman again.'

'I'm pleased for you.'

They sipped their coffees.

'Oh, he brought his mother round to see me.'

'I thought you were going to meet her in some neutral place the first time?'

'So did I, but they were passing and Simon just turned up with her.'

Holly frowned. 'That was a bit inconsiderate of him, wasn't it?'

Cathy looked thoughtful.

'I would have preferred to have had some notice, be prepared, but, no, it was fine… really.'

'I wonder why he did that,' mused Holly, frowning.

'I don't know… but anyway… she was very interested in me and Jason, really attentive. She asked me all kinds of questions. She was a bit overwhelming I suppose, but in a nice way.'

'Apart from that, what did you think of her?'

'She was smartly dressed and well spoken, charming really.'

'So you liked her?'

'Yes, I did. I think we could get along just fine.'

Holly sat forward and poured more coffee.

'How was Simon towards his mother?'

'He seemed OK. He left the room actually, he made the tea.'

'Did she know much about you and Jason?'

'Yes, she did seem to know quite a lot, but that's good, isn't it?'

'Did she talk to you about Simon when he was out of the room?'

'No, she just focused on me, which was really nice. She even offered to babysit at the weekend so I could go rock climbing!'

'That's a little premature. You wouldn't, would you?'

'Wouldn't what?'

'Let her babysit?'

'No, I don't know her well enough yet but it might be

handy in the future. I don't want my rock- climbing days to be over, I do miss it.'

'You could ask me.'

'Yes, I know, but it was kind of her to offer.'

'I think it's strange she offered when she hasn't even met Jason and doesn't know you.'

'But it was nice of her, don't you think?' Cathy rubbed her chin. 'Look, what do you think, Holly? Tell me! I sense you're not that sure about him.'

'To be honest, it seems that there might be a future there for you both, but I don't feel I've met the true Simon yet.'

Cathy frowned. 'What do you mean?'

'I would like to get to know him better before I pass judgement.'

'Why is that?'

Holly finished her coffee then put the cup on the table.

'I've only met him once; it takes a long time to get to know someone accurately in my opinion.'

'He was probably just a bit inhibited meeting you. Look, thanks for looking after my interests but I don't think you need to be suspicious. How about if I arrange for you and George to come round for supper, although God knows what I'll cook. Don't expect cordon bleu.'

'That's a good idea... and I eat out enough. On this occasion I really don't care about the banquet. I'd like to meet him in a more relaxed setting. Maybe when he's had a few glasses of wine any inhibitions will simple dissolve away.'

'You're not planning to get him drunk, are you?'

'No, just enough to loosen his tongue, get him to slip off his Yves St Laurent jumper and see what's underneath that sophisticated façade, that's all.'

Cathy raised her eyes heavenwards. 'Really!'

'Now, when would be a good time?'

'I'll talk to Simon and see when is good for him and let

you know.'

    'Likewise, I'll talk to George.'

    'Let's hope it's soon.'

CHAPTER 10

'He's a great lad.' Simon leaned across the crisp linen tablecloth and took Cathy's hands in his. In the fading twilight his face was lit up with a soft glow and he stared affectionately into her eyes.

'Do you think so? He can be quite a handful.'

Orchestral mood music played lightly in the background; the atmosphere in the restaurant was intimate and snug. She looked around at the other couples talking quietly, holding hands. He's chosen such a nice place, she thought.

'He's a likeable boy, and a real character. I'm fond of him. How does he like being back at school after the long summer?'

'He's fine. He's made some new friends already. His new class teacher, Mrs Morgan, seems nice. She's approachable and Jason likes her, which is the really important thing. He seems much more settled,' she looked away coyly, 'since you came into our lives actually.'

He smiled warmly at her. 'It's nice of you to say so.'

'And it was nice of you to take us to the match.'

'I enjoyed it, and I liked having him with us. I think he's become a Chelsea supporter now,' chuckled Simon.

'Looks like it, but they are a winning team so a good one to back.'

'It wasn't too boring for you, was it?'

'Excuse me.' A waitress leant over and lit the candle on their table.

'Thanks,' said Simon.

The waitress smiled at them, 'You're welcome,' and backed away.

'I'm not that keen on football, but it was great seeing

Jason so happy, especially when you bought him the ice cream and chips. His whole face lit up, even if he did feel sick afterwards.' She giggled.

'Now you're not going to get punitive with me, are you?' Simon winked at her. 'He said you don't like him eating, how he did he describe it, "rubbish" food.'

'No, as it was a treat, I'll let you off this time,' she said cheerfully. 'He'll have had a healthy meal tonight though, I've left him a cheese salad followed by strawberry yoghurt. I hope he's eaten it.'

'Why shouldn't he? Does he still get unsettled when we go out?'

'Only if he doesn't know the babysitter.'

'This is Karen, isn't it?'

'That's right.'

'I think he's had her before.'

'Yes, once.'

'Let's hope there are no problems then.'

'Yes, it is nice going out with you, and with Jason settled it's even better.' She smiled coyly at him.

After a thoughtful moment he stared searchingly into her eyes. 'Has there been anyone else, anyone special who's taken you out?'

'No.' She shook her head. 'I haven't been looking. Up until now all my energy has gone into Jason.'

'No one?'

'I did date a couple of "frogs" before you, through the agency, but Jason is the only person I've cuddled, been intimate with, for years.'

'Then I'm such a lucky guy.' He smiled at her tenderly.

'Thank you for saying so. This is a new adventure for me.'

'And I hope proving a good one.'

'Football, dining at different places, pubs, pub gardens, cinema, stately homes, windmills. A whole new world is opening up.'

'When was the last time you went to the theatre?'

She looked up at the ceiling. 'Hmm… I think it was… *Watford Palace Theatre*, about fifteen years ago… to see a pantomime. Yes. That's it.'

'Funny you should say that. That's the very theatre I thought I'd take you to. They've got an Alan Ayckbourn play coming on soon. It's one of my favourites, *Absurd Person Singular*, I'm sure you'll like it.'

'Oh, how lovely. Yes, please. I don't know much about that writer, but I'll look forward to it.'

'Now I'm here I hope you'll do a lot more things with me that you wouldn't otherwise have done. It's so much nicer doing things together. Don't you agree?'

'Yes, it is.'

Cathy withdrew her hands, sat back and took a sip of her wine.

'I'm fond of children, though I don't suppose I'll have any of my own now. Still, looking after someone like Jason instead – well, it's almost as good.'

'That's nice,' mused Cathy. 'You're quite an unusual man I think.'

People moved about in the restaurant creating soft currents of air; the candle on their table flickered gently.

'Boys do need a father figure in their lives, in my opinion anyway. All the same, you're doing a great job as a single mum.'

Cathy sighed. 'Well, needs must, but, to be honest, I'd prefer it if you didn't call me a single mum. I get it all the time. I don't like being defined by it.'

Simon looked up to the ceiling for a moment, considering.

'OK, fabulous mother to Jason, how's that?'

'That's better, although I'm not sure I'm that great, I just do my best.'

She twisted the stem of her glass between her thumb and index finger. The sun having set, in the muted candlelight Simon appeared more handsome than she had noticed before.

He looked thoughtful for a moment.

'I don't like to pry, but you're OK... financially I mean? You said you own the flat, and it's a very nice one, but you can't earn a huge salary working part-time.'

Cathy stiffened.

'I'm all right, really, I'm fortunate, I've got enough.'

His face expressed compassion, but at the same time his eyes were somewhat cold and she had difficulty interpreting his feelings. 'I'm glad for you... but money isn't everything of course.' He scratched his chin.

'No, it definitely isn't.'

Simon hesitated, catching her eye briefly before looking away. Then he looked deep into her eyes as he said softly, 'What did happen to Jason's dad? Jason mentioned him, which quite surprised me. He said he'd never met his father; he died a long time ago.'

Cathy felt a wave of heat flood her body. She cupped her face in her hands. 'Please don't ask me. I find it very painful to talk about, even now.'

'Yes, of course, I was wrong to ask. I don't want to upset you, my darling Cathy. You're special to me, you know. I have to admit that I've met lots of girls through the agency but you're the only one I can say that about.' He took a deep breath, scanned the room and sitting forward he reached for her hand, stroking it tenderly. 'I'm sorry, forgive me.' His face wore an expression of sincerity that made her feel safe and loved.

'I enjoy being with you,' said Cathy. 'And you've been very kind. To both of us.'

Simon nodded. 'I just don't see enough of you and Jason though. It's this blasted job of mine getting in the way.'

'Yes, it is a shame we can't see more of you.'

'But it doesn't have to be this way. Can you see a future for us together, Cathy? A committed future? I certainly can. I've thought about this over the last few weeks and I believe we can make each other very happy.' Quietly he said, 'You know, I really think I love you, Cathy.'

CHAPTER 11

Cathy poured boiling water over the teabag and splashed a dash of milk into the cup before answering the telephone.

'Cathy, darling.'

'Hello, Mummy, how are you?'

'About the same, I'm well enough.' Cathy could hear the hesitation in her mother's voice. 'It's Bradley. I know I shouldn't complain. I have enough to be thankful for, but he is deteriorating.'

'Hang on, Mummy,' said Cathy, 'I'm just going to pick up this call in the living room.'

Cathy carried her cup of tea into the living room and settled down into the sofa, ready for a long conversation. She picked up the telephone receiver. 'OK, I'm here now,' she said. 'I'm sorry to hear Bradley's getting worse. Is there something in particular?'

'His mobility... it's very limited now. He can hardly stand to transfer to his armchair. I'm developing muscles in all sorts of unlikely places.'

'You shouldn't be taking his weight, he could fall on you, then where will we be?'

'I know. I've applied for assistance with transfers and toileting. I've been told there's a community support team and he'll be allocated a case worker, someone to pop in a couple of times a day, but it all takes time.'

'Please take care. What about his daughter, Charlotte, she lives nearby, doesn't she?'

'Yes, but she works. She's got a new job, teaching at the further education college. Now that the new academic year has started she's not so available. She's always there in an emergency though, when I need her.'

'That's a relief.'

'Talking of the new academic year, Jason must be back at school now.'

'Yes, he's been back a week.'

'Is it going well?'

'Yes, fine.'

'Good. Anyway, I just wish you and Jason lived nearby.'

Cathy sighed. 'I wasn't the one who went to live in Canada, Mummy.'

'Oh, don't remind me. But it's impossible for me to visit you at the moment, however much I want to. I'm completely trapped.'

'I know.'

Cathy heard her mother clear her throat.

'Look, I've been thinking about you and the young man, Simon, you mentioned you'd been seeing. It's been a long time since you've talked about there being anyone. How is it going?'

'It's going well. Jason really likes him.'

'He likes children?'

'Yes, but he doesn't have any of his own.'

'What's his background? Tell me all about him. I'm just sorry I'm not going to be able to meet him.'

Cathy gave a comprehensive summary of everything she knew about Simon.

'So he wants to set up his own business?'

'Yes.'

'Doing what, exactly?'

'Repairs, apparently. Electrical items, TVs, toasters, stereo systems, heaters, all sorts of domestic appliances for households and small businesses. That sort of thing.'

'He'll need some sort of office and workspace, won't he?'

'Yes, he's talked about it.'

'And when does he want to do this?'

'I don't know, he didn't really say, but when he does he'll be settled in one place and we'll see more of him.'

'So he's thinking about a long-term future for you both?'

Cathy smiled quietly to herself. 'Yes, he is, for us all; Jason is part of this, in fact central to it. It couldn't be any other way.'

'Of course, but putting Jason aside, how do *you* feel about him?'

Cathy took a sip of tea.

'Well, he pays me lots of attention, he's always considerate and reliable, except when he's called away by work at short notice, but he always lets me know. He gets quite fed up about it when that does happen.'

'So he has some good qualities, but what are his weaknesses as you see them? You must be realistic; he must have some.'

'Well, not many, happily.' Cathy hesitated. 'He is just a little bit concerned about his appearance, I suppose.'

'In what way?'

'He pays a lot of attention to his looks and how others view him.'

'Well, that might be good if he's in business.'

'I suppose, but sometimes I think it's a bit over the top.'

'So he's vain?'

'Well, I wouldn't call it that. That would be a bit negative… Holly has met him as well and she liked him. You remember Holly, she's suspicious of everybody.'

'Yes, of course I remember Holly. A bright girl, and I expect she's a good judge of character.'

'She wants to get to know him better.'

'Good for her. I trust her opinion. Does he have any brothers or sisters?'

'No, he's an only child.'

'And his parents, have you met them?'

'Yes, he brought his mother round to meet me. His parents split up when he was about twelve, sadly. He hasn't seen his father since.'

'That's a shame. What was the mother like?'

'Oh, very nice. Very smartly dressed. Like him I suppose, nicely spoken, charming. I'm sure we'll get along.'

'And he has money set aside to buy a house you said, but he doesn't own one at the moment.'

'That's right.'

Cathy sipped some more tea.

'Is he enriching your life? Be honest, are you sure you'd be happier with him rather than without him? Look to the future, darling.'

'Yes, I really think so. I always look forward to him coming. I don't feel so lonely anymore and it's nice being able to share things with him, particularly about Jason.'

'You know, this all sounds quite promising. There's nothing I'd like more than to see you and Jason settled.' Cathy heard her mother sigh. 'But is he the one?'

Cathy pulled her feet up underneath her on the sofa and sipped her tea reflectively.

'Darling, are you there?'

'Yes... you know, Mummy, given the timing and Jason growing up and everything, I think he might be.'

'Well, I hope you're not going just to live with him. I'd like to see you committed in the long term, you know, married. I really think this would be best for Jason.'

'Yes, so do I. When I get married, if I do, I want to be as happy as you and Dad were.'

She heard her mother chuckle down the end of the phone.

'It didn't come that easy, you know. You have to work at it, darling.'

'I know, I would be prepared for that, for compromises

and challenges, but it would definitely be worth it to be in a committed partnership. I think marriage is special; well, it should be.'

'I suppose he hasn't asked you yet then?'

'There have been hints.'

'Well, if he does, take your time, don't rush into anything.'

'You know what, Mummy?'

'Yes?'

'I think if he asks I might say yes. I'm not getting any younger.'

'If you're sure of him.'

'I'm as sure in the circumstances as I could be. You know, after Jason's dad... '

'What?'

Cathy bit her lip. 'Well, it's difficult, but I can't expect anyone to be perfect.' The doorbell went. She looked at her watch. 'Look, we've been on the phone so long I've forgotten about the time.'

'Just let me say one thing. You know I think about you a lot. I'm sorry I haven't always been there for you in the way you would wish and I regret that. When you were having a hard time I was focusing on myself and Bradley, well, too much and I'm sorry you weren't able to talk to me.'

'It's all right, I understand.'

'We were estranged for much too long and I'm sorry about it. Very sorry.'

'Yes, it was hard.'

'But I want to be there for you now.'

'Thanks, that's so good to know. Look, there's someone at the door. It's probably Simon. He's taken the afternoon off. I need to go.'

'OK, darling. Goodbye now and keep in touch. Oh, and if you have a photo of him, please send it to me.'

'Sure, I'll look one out. Bye, Mummy.'

'Bye, darling.'

As Cathy opened the door to Simon, she caught a whiff of his aftershave. He stood straight and stiff, his arms folded across his chest.

'I thought you weren't in,' he said, frowning.

'Sorry for the delay, my mother's been on the phone.'

'Your mother Anna, in Canada?'

'Yes. We don't talk very often but when we do it takes an age catching up. She does show a lot of interest in Jason though and I am grateful for that. It wasn't always that way.'

'You know, I'd like to have a chat with her on the phone sometime.'

'Yes, good idea.'

He followed her down the corridor.

'Tea, coffee, wine? What would you like?' She looked him up and down. 'Are they new clothes you're wearing? They look nice.'

'I bought this new shirt and trousers only the other day. Glad you noticed.'

'What can I get you?' She stood facing him, waiting for his reply.

His expression was awkward somehow. He half smiled, dipped his hand into his canvas shopping bag, and pulled out a bottle.

'I think this might be in order.'

'Oh, wine?'

'No, champagne,' he said with a confident flourish.

'Oh, are we celebrating something?'

'I hope so.' He took a deep breath and held his hand out, grabbing hers. 'Here, come into the living room.' He led the way. 'Here.' He patted a space on the sofa and indicated for her to sit down.

She sat; her mind was racing. Simon knelt down and

79

looked into her eyes for a few moments, his expression inscrutable.

'Well, as your father is dead and your mother is in Canada I have no one else to consult, so I will ask you directly.'

He dipped into his pocket and pulled out a small leather-bound box fastened with a clasp. Cathy looked, her eyes wide, her heart thumping a little. He paused, savouring the special moment, then slowly opened the box. She saw inside a small ring, a dark blue gem surrounded with glittering crystals.

'This is for you, Cathy, you must know why. I want you to be my wife.' He lifted it out and placed it on her finger.

She gasped and put her hand to her chest. 'It fits so well, a perfect size.' Cathy's voice trembled a little. 'How did you do it?'

'I borrowed one of your other rings for size when you weren't looking.'

'You did?' She studied her hand for a few moments. 'It's beautiful.'

'It's a sapphire surrounded by diamonds. Sapphire is my favourite colour. I thought this one would suit your small delicate hand.' He took her hand and kissed each finger.

'It looks wonderful.'

'Well, Cathy darling, what do you say?'

She took a deep breath, feeling her eyes moisten.

'Oh Simon, it's such a surprise. I... I... don't know what to say.'

'I hope I've done enough to convince you I'll be a good husband to you and a good father to Jason.'

Her eyes wet, she looked at him and blinked.

'Yes, of course you have.'

'I love you, Cathy, I know that now.' He looked into her eyes, his expression full of anticipation and confidence.

She hesitated for only a moment. 'I love you too. Yes, of course I'll marry you.'

She hugged him.

CHAPTER 12

'Are you nervous?' asked Holly.

'A bit,' Cathy admitted, smoothing her dress for the umpteenth time. 'I so want it all to go right.'

'It'll be fine, I promise you. I'll keep Jason with me, so you don't have to worry about him. Just focus on Simon. And the registrar, of course.'

'What do you think about my wedding dress? I know it's not the simple one you and I picked out.'

'Was there something wrong with that one? You looked divine in it.'

'Well, Margaret thought it wasn't stylish enough and showed a bit too much cleavage. She discussed it with Simon and they persuaded me to swap it. Margaret helped me choose this one. Do you like it?'

Holly forced herself to look again at Cathy in the off-the-shoulder, belted dress, with the voluminous skirt that swamped her. 'You look gorgeous. I hope Simon realises what a lucky chap he is, marrying you. Talking of marrying, we'd better get going or you'll be late.'

A short time later their taxi drew up outside Watford Register Office and Cathy and Holly clambered out and went inside the nondescript red brick building.

Upstairs, Holly could see Simon was smartly dressed in a grey suit, navy tie and black patent shoes. He was standing outside a door halfway down the carpeted corridor, talking animatedly to a tall, slim, dark-haired woman in a low-cut, tight-fitting blue dress. Simon seems to have no problem with the amount of cleavage she's showing, thought Holly. And he's standing quite a bit closer to her than he should, as well. Jason was sitting on a padded chair, looking bored. He wore a white shirt with a red bow-tie and a pair of brown trousers. Next to him sat an older woman, extravagantly dressed. This must be Margaret, Simon's mother, thought Holly. Simon looked up as he saw them approach and smiled affectionately.

'Cathy,' he said, looking her up and down. He gave her a hug and a light kiss on the lips. 'You look fabulous. Doesn't she, Mother?'

'Definitely,' said Margaret, getting to her feet. 'What a lovely dress we chose.'

Simon looked over at Holly and said quietly, 'No offence, Holly, but Mother is always so right about what suits people.'

Holly took a deep breath, but said nothing.

'And I've never seen Simon look as handsome as he does today,' said Margaret. 'You're such an attractive young couple.' She carefully adjusted Simon's tie and gave Cathy a weak hug before looking back affectionately at Simon. 'I'm so happy that you and Simon are getting married.'

As Holly watched the scene unfold she had an uncomfortable feeling of foreboding.

'Mother, this is Holly, Cathy's friend,' said Simon.

'Pleased to meet you, especially on such a special day,' said Holly.

Holly decided that Margaret's bright pink dress with matching bolero jacket and skyhigh fascinator looked a bit too gaudy and inappropriate for such an understated wedding.

'Oh, isn't it, October 20th, this auspicious date that I shall never forget in all the years to come,' said Margaret exuberantly. 'Seeing Simon happily settled and moving on with his life is very special indeed; I've been hoping for this day for a very long time. And Cathy will make such a lovely wife, of course.'

'Cathy, dear, this is Rachel,' said Simon, indicating the

83

dark-haired woman. 'She's a temp, working in one of the offices here. She's agreed to be the other witness, with Holly.'

'Pleased to meet you,' said Cathy, shaking Rachel's hand.

'Best of luck,' said Rachel.

'Thank you.' Cathy squatted down, hugged Jason and gave him a peck on the cheek. 'Hello, darling. Are you OK?'

'Can we go home now, Mummy?' asked Jason.

'No, darling, I told you before you came down here with Simon. Mummy and Simon are going to get married and then later we'll go back home together, as a family. You'll like that, won't you?'

Jason nodded and grinned.

The door opened and an official-looking, tall, brown-haired man wearing a smart grey suit came out.

'Sorry for the delay,' he said, 'I was just checking some paperwork. My name is Lawson, I'm the registrar on duty. Do come in, and we'll get started.'

As they filed into the room, Holly saw several rows of folding wooden chairs set out, with a small cushion on each seat. There was a long plain wooden table, with two ledgers open on it, at the back of the room. Four chairs were arranged along one side of the table. At both ends of the table there was a wooden floor stand, each holding a vase of crimson and orange lilies. Holly could smell their sweet aroma as soon as she stepped inside. Light flooded in through a large picture window set in the back wall. Holly took Jason's hand and sat him down beside her on a chair in the front row. Margaret settled herself on the other side of Jason and Rachel sat beside Margaret.

After the short ceremony, with Cathy and Simon exchanging vows and rings, Mr Lawson said, 'You are now husband and wife. Congratulations.'

84

Simon gave Cathy a lingering kiss, as Holly, Margaret and Rachel applauded. Jason watched with a bemused expression.

'Simon and Cathy, would you please sit at the table and we'll do the signing of the registers,' said Lawson. He placed one of the ledgers in front of Simon and handed him a fountain pen. 'Would you sign here, please,' he said, indicating the line in the register. After Simon had signed, Lawson put the second register in front of him and again indicated the place to sign. Lawson repeated the process with Cathy. 'Now the witnesses, please,' he said.

Simon and Cathy got up and Holly and Rachel took their places. Holly saw Simon move to one side slightly, looking down. Suddenly she had the horrible realisation that he'd moved to where he could get a better view down Rachel's front. The bastard! she thought. He's only been married two minutes and he's already on the prowl. She groaned inwardly: what should she tell Cathy, if anything? Summoning up as much cheerfulness as she could, she congratulated Cathy and Simon and wished them all the happiness in the world. Inside, her heart sank.

CHAPTER 13

Simon took off his shoes and called from the hallway, 'Hello, darling, I'm home.'

'Oh, you're nice and early.' Cathy strode briskly towards him and gave him a peck on the cheek and a hug. 'How did you manage to get away?'

'I arranged that the last client was a short drive away. I wanted to be at home with you and Jason as early as I could.'

Simon placed his shoes neatly by the front door and hung up his coat.

'Lovely, maybe you could do that all the time.'

'When I can, when I haven't got hothead Dobson breathing down my neck,' he grimaced. 'He's gone away for a few days, thank God, so I can be more flexible with my appointments. I've been missing you so much.' He looked her up and down and took her hands in his. 'You know, I've been thinking... '

'Yes?'

'Do you always have to wear those dowdy old clothes around the house? It would be nice to see you in something stylish sometimes.'

Cathy gave a short laugh of incredulity. 'These are my slopping-around-comfort clothes. They're just right for home. Why would I want to wear something "stylish" as you put it?'

'For me.'

Cathy put her hands on her hips. 'Oh, you are funny. If we ever go out somewhere really special I promise to wear a frock. OK?' she said cheerfully.

'OK, darling. Anyway, I'll change out of this suit.'

'You do that, something sloppy please,' she grinned at

him. 'I'm just cooking.'

Ten minutes later Simon went into the kitchen and flopped onto an aluminium chair. 'It's so nice coming home to you and Jason rather than my mother.'

'Glad you feel like that, we'd be in trouble if you didn't.'

'Now I feel I have a family of my own.'

'Yes, it's lovely.' Cathy passed him a cup of tea. 'I'm so glad you're here.'

'Me too.' He relaxed back, stretched his arms above his head and stared at the ceiling for a few moments. 'I really want to spend more time with Jason.'

Cathy stood at the worktop, chopping tomatoes, lettuce and celery.

'It's a good start. Your first day at work after our honeymoon and you're home early.'

'It was such a good trip. You did like the place I chose, didn't you?'

'Yes, of course. I've always liked Devon and their beaches and cream teas. We were so lucky with the weather. It's difficult to believe it's autumn.'

'Yes, and now I really must get down to setting up my own business.'

'We're only just married, there's plenty of time. Let's be settled first, as a family. It's best for Jason I think.'

'Well, I want to get a move on with this.'

'And talking of Jason.' She stopped what she was doing and stood there with a stalk of celery in one hand and a small chopping knife in the other, her back to the sink. 'I've been planning on setting up a savings fund for him for some time now.'

'Good idea.'

'So, I wondered, now you're here, maybe you wouldn't mind helping towards the bills; you did offer, remember?'

'Did I?'

'You know, the gas, electric, rates. I've just about managed to pay them until now but it would allow me to squirrel this money away for Jason.'

'Hmm... I vaguely remember you telling me about this plan, but just to be clear, there's no other loan or anything outstanding, on the flat, for instance?'

She cleared her throat. 'No, there's nothing to pay on the flat, only the bills.'

He studied her for a few moments as she made a salad dressing.

'Of course as your husband I want to help, but I'm saving up for the new business venture at the moment. Give me a few months, then I'll happily contribute. You've managed up until now, haven't you?'

She frowned. 'Yes, it's just for Jason.'

'Once the business takes off there'll be plenty of money, don't you worry.' He sniffed. 'Anyway, when is Edward's mother bringing him home?'

'About 6.30, after the party.'

'I hope he's not too tired to play with the new train set I bought him.'

'Be prepared, he gets grumpy when he's tired.' Cathy finished making the salad and sat opposite him.

'You know, there's a very nice smell that's making me hungry. What are you cooking?'

'Cottage pie with side salad.'

'Sounds and smells wonderful.'

'Oh, I've just remembered, Holly says she's passing by on Saturday morning and she'd like to drop in, spend some time with both of us at last. It's such a shame we never managed to get her and George round for dinner that time. She thinks she hardly knows you.'

Simon groaned and frowned. 'Oh no, Cathy, let's be together on our own.'

Cathy was silent for a moment, then shrugged. 'OK...

it's just that it's really difficult for her to find time to see us.'

'Anyway, to be honest, I think Holly's a bit overbearing, isn't she.'

'Oh, what do you mean?'

'She's used to being in charge.'

Cathy frowned. 'She's been nothing but supportive to me, to us.'

'Be honest now, *interfering* is more accurate.'

Cathy bristled. 'I don't think so; you're doing her an injustice. She was wonderful looking after Jason when we were away. That was very helpful of her and she took annual leave to do it.'

'You bought her flowers, didn't you, as a thank you, and she enjoys being with Jason. It's no hardship for her, in fact the opposite.'

'She's fond of Jason... '

'I understand that but he needs to get to know me now. One day, I hope, I'll be able to call him my son.'

'Your son?'

'Come on, we have touched on it, Cathy; I want to formally adopt him, then we'll be a proper family.'

He leant over and took her hand. 'It's your choice, of course, there's no hurry, but we do need to spend time together, just the three of us.'

He held her gaze.

'Yes, I see what you mean.'

'Put Holly off will you, just this once, until we're settled.'

Cathy shrugged. 'OK then.'

'Talking about being settled... Mother's talking about moving and what to do with my furniture... I don't expect she'll move for a while though, it'll take her ages to make up her mind.'

He got up, walked round to her side of the table,

squatted down and cuddled her. Looking into her eyes he said: 'It's wonderful being married. You're such a wonderful girl, I mean woman, lady.' They kissed. 'You taste delicious, let me see, cottage pie? All those teaspoons of tasters I expect.' They giggled. 'You know what, with just a bit of practice I think you're going to be a very good cook.'

'Don't bank on it.'

'Anyway, you've done enough working, you need a break, a treat. I'd like to take my wonderful new wife out to dinner on Saturday; Mother said she'll come and babysit.'

'Did she? That's nice of her. Where are we going?'

'To *The Angus Steak House*.'

'Oh, I've never been there before. Do they do anything other than steak? I know you like it but it's not my favourite.'

'Yes, I was thinking of you as well of course; they do some really tasty salads and pastas.'

'Ok, thank you. As long as there's something for me to eat.'

He fiddled with her long floppy jumper.

'None of these dowdy clothes, OK? You're married to me now... a married woman. You should have more confidence. When was the last time you put on make-up and perfume, apart from our wedding day of course?'

'Look, it's because I'm confident that I don't need smart clothes and perfume.'

'But it's nice for me if you look glamorous in public. And it pleases me to see you looking your best, even at home.'

'Do you really need me to?'

'I don't need you to, I love you just as you are, but it would be nice.'

He stroked her cheek and kissed her again.

CHAPTER 14

'That's all I bloody need,' said Simon into the telephone. 'The boiler's packed up. No hot water and no heating.'

'Well,' said his mother at the other end of the line, 'find a plumber then.'

'Don't have time, I'm due at an important client's site this morning, in fact I'm running late as it is.'

'What about Cathy? Surely she can use a telephone?'

'She's gone with Jason on a school trip. Left about 7am to catch the coach. The boiler was still working then but it's been playing up for weeks.'

'Well, you do need a plumber.'

'Oh, I remember, there's a sticker on the side of the boiler, I'll go and have a look. Just a minute.'

Simon went to the kitchen then a few minutes later returned to the telephone.

'Yes, I've got the name and telephone number of a plumber. He must have been here before.'

'Give me the details. I'll call.'

'Thanks, Mother. Tell him it's an emergency – I need him here this afternoon. I should be back by 4.30.'

'All right, dear, what's his number?'

'It's 0181 555 8972, and his name's Ricardo Maretti. He should be able to fix it; he serviced it in January, there's a date on the sticker. Disgraceful it's packed up already.'

'Let's hope it's not shoddy workmanship, darling. Anyway, I'll ring him straightaway and won't take no for an answer.'

'Thanks, Mother. Gotta dash. Bye.' Simon grabbed his coat and sped out of the flat, slamming the door behind him.

When he returned later that afternoon, the red light on

the answering machine was flashing insistently. Impatiently he pressed the Play button.

'Hello, dear,' said his mother's voice, 'I spoke to Ricardo's mother. She said she would pass the message on to him. I stressed the urgency of the situation and she said he would definitely leave a message for you later this morning. Good luck.' There was a click and a whirr from the machine as it played the next message.

'Cathy,' came a man's voice, 'is Ricardo. Mama told me you rang. Thought you forgotten me. So sorry boiler he not work. I come fix, today, just for you. I be there five o'clock maybe.'

Frowning, Simon played the message again. '"Forgotten me", "just for you", eh?' he muttered, before stabbing his finger on the Delete button, erasing Ricardo. He looked at his watch: 4.20pm. In the bedroom, Simon changed out of his work clothes, putting on a pair of grey chinos and a pale blue Ralph Lauren polo shirt. He went into the kitchen and made a cheese sandwich and a mug of coffee before settling himself at the kitchen table. He leafed desultorily through the day's newspaper. Just after 5.15pm the doorbell rang. Simon folded the newspaper and went to the front door. He peeped through the spyhole and saw a black-haired man with olive skin who had a wide grin on his face. As Simon opened the door and swung it wide, Ricardo's grin vanished, replaced by a puzzled expression.

'Cathy?' he said hesitantly.

'Cathy's not here,' said Simon.

'She call me this morning,' said Ricardo, 'her boiler, he no work. I come fix.'

'It was my mother that called you,' said Simon. 'But yes, the boiler is not working. You'd better come and have a look at it.'

'Your mother? Not Cathy? She move out?' Ricardo

looked downcast.

'No, Cathy's away just for the day. Now are you going to look at the boiler or not?'

'Yes, I come,' Ricardo said despondently. He picked up his bulging toolbag and with head down reluctantly followed Simon along the corridor to the kitchen. Thirty minutes later he knocked on the living-room door.

'Well?' snapped Simon.

'Boiler he work now.'

'About time,' said Simon. 'You serviced it earlier this year, it shouldn't have stopped working. What was wrong with it?'

'Valve stuck. Sometime new valve he have too small grease. I put much more. Work easy now. All done.'

'What's the damage?'

Ricardo looked puzzled again. 'No, he not damaged. I fix.'

'I mean, how much is the bill?'

'Very not much. Thirty pounds.'

Simon counted out three ten-pound notes from his wallet. 'Here,' he said. 'Off you go.'

'You want receipt?'

'No, just clear off. You're no longer needed here.' Simon looked Ricardo steadily in the eye.

'I go.' Ricardo let himself out and walked down the stairs, his shoulders slumped. Simon went into the kitchen and strode over to the boiler. He ripped off Ricardo's card from the side, tore it into small pieces and flung it into the bin. 'No one for five years, huh?' he muttered under his breath.

CHAPTER 15

'Hi, Simon, you've just beaten me,' called Cathy as she climbed the stairs carrying a bag of groceries.

'Hi, darling. Is that dinner you've got there?'

'It might be if you're lucky,' she chuckled.

'How was the office today?' he said, looking somewhat awkward.

'It was busy, then Maurice had some urgent paperwork and asked me to stay late. The deadline is November 30th, three days' time. Jason's gone to supper with Charlie. His mum will bring him home later.'

Simon opened the front door to the flat and they stepped into the hallway.

'Oh,' she said, looking down the corridor, 'What's all this?' Once a wide, uncluttered area, there were now boxes piled up high, a ceramic-topped coffee table and a huge Welsh dresser. There was a musty smell.

'This is my furniture that I've been storing at my mother's house. You don't mind, do you? She's getting rid of things, insisting I take what's mine, in preparation for her eventual move to a flat.'

'I wish you'd warned me. Is this all of it or is there more to come?'

'No, that's the lot.'

She put her shopping bag down and looked around.

'Come and see the dresser,' said Simon.

He took her by the hand and led her down the corridor. They stopped in front of the imposing piece of furniture. It looked substantial, made of dark mahogany. There were several sets of shelves for displaying plates and underneath were some drawers. 'My grandmother left it to me when she died,' Simon said. He stroked the smooth polished wood.

'Well, as a piece of furniture it's nice I suppose but it's huge and takes up so much space. I don't want it here, Simon. Can't your mother take it back?'

'It took four burly men to get it upstairs. I guess I could arrange for it to be collected and shipped back to Mother's house but when she moves we'll be in the same situation.'

Cathy huffed. 'Well, it's not right here.'

'Unless... we could move it into the spare room but there's already a table and some chairs in there.'

'Oh my goodness, how much stuff have you moved in? You said this was it.'

'Well, it's all my stuff.' He scratched the back of his neck. 'I've had it for donkey's years; come on, Cathy, there's plenty of room here.' Simon followed as Cathy walked down the corridor to the spare room. There was a square G-Plan table with formica top in the middle of the room, with four collapsible chairs arranged around it. 'These will all fold up flat so the dresser will fit in here nicely.'

'I suppose so.' She swallowed hard. 'It's just – I'm used to having this room clear, empty.'

'But why? It's wasted space, isn't it? Be honest.'

'I don't need a lot of furniture. I... I can't explain.' Cathy sucked in a deep breath as she remembered Blake standing shirtless in the empty space on that fateful day, that special cherished moment. She pinched herself and put her hands on her hips. 'Well, what else is there apart from everything in the hallway?'

'My wardrobe. I've put it in our bedroom. You know I needed more hanging space. Come and see it.'

In the bedroom stood a large pine wardrobe with a mirror on each of the three panels. It took up most of the space in front of one wall. 'Where's my wicker chair gone?' asked Cathy. 'It used to be there, where the wardrobe is.'

'I put it in the kitchen. It's more comfortable than the aluminium ones.'

'I see.' Cathy frowned. 'But I liked it there; I used it when I was dressing.'

'I'll bring a kitchen chair in instead, OK?'

'I suppose... '

'There's not too much, is there? Anyway, you'll get used to it and it makes me feel even more at home, having my own things around me.' Simon pulled Cathy to him, gave her a bear-hug and kissed her tenderly on the cheek. 'Now it's *our* home.' They stood there silently for a few moments as he rocked her gently back and forwards, stroking her hair, but she felt stiff. I mustn't feel this resentment, it's wrong, she thought, I need to share my life, I must be accommodating, it will strengthen the marriage, enrich it. I've been on my own too long, set in my own ways.

'Darling, I've just had an idea about something else.' He took her hand.

'What is it?'

'Look up, at the ceiling.'

'There's nothing there, just plaster, painted white. What am I supposed to see?'

'Yes, just a plain, boring ceiling. But what if we put a mirror up there, above the bed?'

'What?'

'We could watch ourselves, making love. I could see your beautiful, toned body from all angles, and we can see each other touching, caressing. Our lovemaking would be even better, if that's possible.'

Cathy flinched. 'No, Simon. I'm too shy for that.'

Simon frowned and looked her steadily in the eye for a long moment.

'I'm not sure about that. In fact I suspect you're not

96

quite as shy as you like to make out.'

'No, you're wrong, Simon. I really don't think so... '

Cathy pushed away from him and took a step back.

'Look, you're married now; you don't need to be inhibited with me. It's been a while, hasn't it? Five years?'

She nodded. 'Yes, more than five years.'

'Honestly? No one at all?'

Cathy stepped back again. 'What do you mean? What are you implying?'

His eyes narrowed. 'There was something funny about the plumber, Ricardo Maretti, when he came the other day.'

Cathy breathed hard and felt her cheeks redden. 'The plumber? Came here? When?'

'Monday evening, three days ago. You know the boiler has been on the blink? Well, it packed up completely. I had to go to a client so my mother phoned and left a message for him to come round urgently. He left a peculiar answer machine message for a tradesman: "I thought you'd forgotten me". You must admit that's not very professional, a strange thing to say. What's going on?'

Cathy stepped back, leaned against the wall, put her hand over her mouth and stood silent for a few moments.

'Why didn't you tell me he'd come, why wait until now? It's my flat, my boiler.'

She hugged herself.

'Our flat. Anyway, that's beside the point. It was a lot to take in. I had to think about it. About what to say to you... that strange message. He was obviously looking forward to seeing you and most put out when I answered the door. He wanted to know where you were.' He looked sharply at her. 'Well?' His tone was challenging.

Cathy felt her heart beat hard in her chest.

'All right, I admit it, I did... It was a one-off, I made a mistake.'

'You went to bed with him?'

She glanced at him briefly and nodded.

'So, my new wife's not as shy, demure and modest as she might lead us to believe.'

Cathy breathed hard. 'As I said, I made a mistake.'

In a sudden outburst he almost spat, 'With the plumber of all people,' his face contorted with contempt and anger. 'How did it happen then, he seduced you? You seduced him? That little squirt of a man, it's contemptible.'

'Please, there's no need to be so angry, it was before I met you.' She retreated into a corner.

Just as quickly he mellowed, his voice soft and reassuring. 'Darling, I'm sorry. I didn't mean to upset you. I really don't care about the plumber. I just want us to have a wonderful future together, which we will have.' He tried to embrace her.

'Not now.' Cathy went to the doorway and into the corridor. 'I need a cup of tea. Will you please tidy these boxes, before Jason comes home.'

'All right, darling.'

Fighting back tears, Cathy made herself a tea and settled down to watch University Challenge on TV. Ten minutes later Simon came and sat down beside her. She shivered.

'I've emptied the boxes; there were books and old study materials mostly, which I want to keep. I've put the boxes out ready for the dustman.'

'Good. There's an unpleasant musty smell though.'

'I can't do anything about that. It's the books I expect.'

'I don't like it.'

'Don't fuss, darling, it's only books. They've been in the garage, some of them. They'll be OK once they've dried out.'

'Hmm... I hope so.'

They watched the programme in silence for a few minutes.

'I never can get any of these questions right,' he said. 'Who do you want to win?'

'Durham. They're a bit behind at the moment but a few right answers and they'll be back in the lead.'

Simon looked at his watch. 'Oh,' he said, 'Money Matters is starting on BBC2 now.' He got up and switched channels. 'You don't mind, do you, darling? It's my favourite programme.' Simon pulled Cathy close and put his arm round her shoulder. 'I'm such a lucky chap, sitting here with my lovely new wife,' he said.

CHAPTER 16

A frail female voice reverberated around the stairwell. 'Cathy, my dear.'

Climbing the staircase, Cathy saw Doreen from the flat opposite standing on the landing; her front door was open. Her thin white hair framed her pinched cheeks and small sunken eyes. She was dressed in a check skirt and thick cardigan. Cathy reached the top of the steps and stood near her.

'Hello, Doreen, how are you? You look cold.'

'I do feel the cold now autumn is here. But I wanted to tell you, I'm going into hospital for a few days. Well, I'm not sure how long really.'

'Oh, I'm sorry, is it your angina again?'

'They want to do tests. I don't know how long I'll be in.'

'Do you want me to look after the flat?'

She shook her head. 'No, but thank you for asking. Alan will be coming in and out.'

'Your son is always very helpful.'

'Yes, he's a good lad. Always looks after me.'

'That must be reassuring.'

'It is. I'm not sure what I'd do without him.'

'Well, let me know how you get on. I hope it will be OK.'

A strange expression crossed Doreen's face. She leant forward and gently grasped Cathy's arm. 'I hope you don't mind me saying,' she lowered her voice, 'but little Jason seems much happier these days. I can hear him singing, and he runs and jumps up the stairs, he's quite changed. He used to be such a shy little boy.'

Cathy smiled. 'Yes, he is happy.'

Doreen put her hand to her ear. 'If I'm not mistaken I can hear him now.'

Cathy heard whoops of delight and laughter from inside the flat.

'Oh yes, so can I,' Cathy said, beaming.

'Bless him; I can see family life is good for him. Such a gentleman, Simon, and always so smart.'

'Er... yes.' Cathy put her key in the lock.

'The little boy needed a father... I was so sorry Blake left... ' She shook her head. 'It was all such a sad business.'

Cathy stopped for a minute and took a deep breath; it was such a long time since she'd heard anyone say his name.

'Very good luck at the hospital,' she said. She turned the key, closed the front door behind her, took off her coat and called, 'Hello, Mummy's home.'

She heard a soft thud, then a giggle. 'Again, again,' said Jason. '1... 2... 3... and... ' There was a soft boom. 'Crash!'

She heard Simon's excited voice. 'You're flying!'

Cathy followed the sound; it was coming from their bedroom. She walked straight in. Jason was standing on the bed.

'Mummy, Mummy, look at our new game, watch!'

Cathy looked around. There was something different about the light in the room but she wasn't quite sure what. Simon stood at the far end of the bed with his knees braced against the mattress. Jason jumped like a monkey on to Simon's chest and clung on. Jason said, '1... 2... 3... ', at which point Simon threw him backwards on to the bed. As Jason landed flat on his back he splayed his arms and legs straight and wide and waved them back and forth. 'Look, Mummy, I'm swimming,' he said and pointed towards the ceiling. Looking up, Cathy shuddered. There, fixed in position directly above the bed, was a gigantic mirror. With horror she realised Jason was looking at his own reflection.

Suddenly he sprang off the bed. 'Let's do it again, Uncle Simon.'

Cathy swallowed hard, her heart beating fast. Jason jumped up on to Simon and the game repeated itself. Simon didn't look at her; he looked only at Jason and the bed, fully absorbed in the game. She felt her cheeks grow hot. She walked straight to the kitchen and stood for a moment. In the distance she could hear them both laughing and joking. She poured herself a neat whisky and stood by the sink looking out of the window at the trees in the garden opposite billowing gently in the wind. She gulped the liquor down in one. Jason ran in and grabbed the sleeve of the woollen jumper she was wearing, pulling her towards the door, his face red and his eyes shining.

'Mummy, you throw me, will you? Join in, Mummy.'

Cathy could barely look at him for fear of showing her feelings. 'Maybe later, darling, I'm tired.'

'OK.' He skipped away.

She stood there in a daze, still watching the trees, trying to grapple with her feelings. After another ten minutes the shouts and screams of delight faded away. She heard the regular clicking of the abacus. The game was obviously over. Simon came up from behind and put his hand on her shoulder. She stiffened.

'It's great seeing Jason so happy, he really enjoyed that.' Cathy didn't respond. She heard him take a deep breath. 'You don't mind, do you, darling, about the mirror? You could call it an early Christmas present if you like, a present for us.' He stood there waiting. She pushed her shoulder back, shrugging him off; his presence felt heavy, disturbing and oppressive. 'We could start with the curtains closed and the lights off until you get used to it.' Still she remained silent. He gently put his arm on her waist from behind and kissed her tenderly on the cheek. 'If you really don't like it we'll have it removed in a few weeks, OK, but let's try it first.'

'I said I didn't want it. You should have asked me first, asked me again. It's my flat, why didn't you ask me first?' she said through gritted teeth.

He was silent for a moment.

'I'm sorry. I thought that if it was there you'd at least give it a try. It's for us, together.'

Cathy swallowed hard again and blinked back tears. 'I don't want it.' She moved away from him and looked over at the pile of clothes waiting to be ironed. 'I'd better get on with these.' She got out the ironing board and lifted it into position.

'I'll do it if you like?' Simon picked up the iron.

Jason stood in the doorway. 'Uncle Simon, come and play with my train set with me, will you?'

'No, you go,' said Cathy.

'You're sure?'

'Yes,' she said brusquely, wanting him away.

Simon went to Jason. Sniffing, Cathy got on with the chore, her mind in turmoil. She tried to stifle the feelings of resentment. With each of his shirts she tugged and pulled the fabric with a bit more force than usual, pressed the iron a bit harder than necessary. Eventually she calmed down and her feelings softened. Maybe I am being a bit prudish, she told herself, and should try. If I'm not happy with it, he'll take it away; he is kind, really. She laboriously ironed and hung up the items of clothing, a mixture of his and hers, one by one.

'Thank you for doing this, darling.' Simon came up close behind her and kissed her on the cheek, watching for a while. 'Oh, you're ironing my shirts inside out I see.'

'Yes, I've always done them like this.'

'Hmm, the problem is the crease in the sleeve looks strange if you do it that way. I have wondered why my shirts looked like they do.'

She bristled. 'It hardly notices, surely.'

'I'm quite particular about my clothes,' he said abruptly. 'Here, let me show you.' He took the shirt and pulled the sleeve the right way out, turned up the steam gauge and smoothed the iron back and forth along the fabric of the sleeve. The iron gurgled and she felt the steam hot against her face.

'Here, this is how I like them done, so in the future you'll do them like this, won't you?' He snuggled into her and his tone softened. 'I love you.'

CHAPTER 17

Cathy swung open the door to her flat. 'Come in, Holly,' she said.

'Darling, I'm so pleased to see you. It's been so long.' She pecked Cathy on the cheek. 'I phoned several times over the last few weeks. I thought you were avoiding me for some reason, not replying to my messages.'

'What messages?'

'I left more than one, with Simon. Didn't he tell you?'

Cathy frowned. 'No, he hasn't said anything at all.'

'How strange.'

Cathy deliberated for a moment. 'It is odd he didn't tell me.' She shrugged. 'I did wonder why I hadn't heard from you. I thought perhaps you were busy or giving us some space as a newlywed couple, something like that.'

'Well, of course I would have done, if you'd said so,' Holly said thoughtfully as she took off her high-heeled boots.

'Simon's been working long hours lately, I think he just wants to be quiet and relax when he gets home.'

Holly scanned Cathy up and down. 'My goodness, is that a dress you're wearing over that jumper?'

Cathy shrugged dismissively. 'It's a pinafore. Simon wants me to wear dresses, thought it might suit me, so this is a compromise.'

'Well, I suppose I'll have to get used to seeing your legs then. Not that they're not nice, in fact they're very nice. Maybe he has got a point.'

'Holly, I hate drawing attention to myself, nice legs or otherwise.'

'I know.'

Holly let out a big sigh.

'You're tired?' asked Cathy.

'Could say that. Now that I've managed to get a few days off work, I'm determined to relax and take it easy. And that starts now. Oh,' she said, noticing the dark mahogany dresser. 'You've been productive in the last month, have you been furniture shopping?'

'No, it's just Simon's stuff. I'll make the coffee.'

Holly walked through to the living room and flopped down onto the sofa, relaxed. Looking around the room, she noticed it seemed different, smaller, darker and more cluttered. There was a heavy ceramic coffee table and a set of book shelves she didn't recognise.

Cathy came in, carrying the coffees and a plate of biscuits on a tray.

'Is this Simon's as well?'

'It seems his mother doesn't want his stuff there. She's moving into a new flat. She needed to move Simon's things out, that's all.'

'Right. You don't mind, having all this extra furniture?' Holly pulled on her long diamanté earring and looked at Cathy.

'It's his,' she sighed.

Jason came running into the room and went straight to Holly. She crouched down and gave him a big hug. 'How's my little friend? Are you on Christmas holidays now?'

'Auntie Holly,' he said, breathlessly. 'Come see my new game.' Jason grabbed Holly's hand and pulled her up from the sofa into Cathy's bedroom. 'Look,' he said, pointing to the ceiling. Holly looked up and saw the large mirror set into the ceiling. Her eyes widened. Jason scrambled onto the bed. '1,2,3 and down!' he shouted, as he flung himself backwards on to the bed, flat on his back. He looked at himself in the ceiling mirror. 'Look, look,' he said, pointing to it with a big grin on his face. 'When I play with Uncle Simon, he *throws* me on the bed.'

'Looks like fun,' said Holly. 'How long have you had this?'

'Don't know. Uncle Simon got it for us. Isn't it great?'

'It's certainly an interesting game, for sure.' She rubbed her chin. 'I'm just going to talk to your Mummy, Jason.'

'OK, I want to play.' He threw himself back on the bed again.

When Holly returned to the living room she found Cathy staring out of the window, her arms crossed. Holly bit her lip. 'Well, darling, he's certainly enjoying himself.' Cathy didn't move or turn around. 'I don't know if you noticed, but he almost dragged me in there.' She cleared her throat. 'I'm sorry; it's a private place, a bedroom. I'll pretend I haven't seen it if you like.'

'What did you think when you saw it?'

Holly cleared her throat. 'Whatever happens between a married couple is their private business, although I don't expect you and Simon play the same game as Jason does.'

Cathy turned around and stared straight at her. 'I didn't want it.'

'The mirror?'

'Yes, the bloody mirror. He mentioned it about three weeks ago; I said I wasn't keen. To stall him, I said I'd think about it. I thought he'd forgotten all about it to be honest. Next thing I knew he'd had it put up while I was out.'

'Bloody cheek! Get him to take it down again, Cathy,' Holly said furiously.

'It's not as easy as all that.'

'He put it up, you don't want it, he takes it down. What could be simpler?'

In the background they could hear Jason counting, '1,2,3... down!'

Cathy took a deep breath and said in a tone of resignation, 'I can't, Jason loves his new game.'

107

'Well, it's not Jason's bloody bedroom, is it?'

'Simon says it will be an adventure, fun, I'll get used to it, given time.'

'And will you?'

'I don't think so.' Cathy glanced at Holly, then looking down, picked at her nails for a few moments. She hid her face in her hands and burst into tears.

Holly took a deep breath. 'Things aren't right here, are they, Cathy?'

'No.' Between sobs she said, 'But you know I've been living on my own... well, with Jason... for such a long time. Maybe I'm just unused to sharing, to compromising.'

Holly came up to her.

'He should be more considerate of your feelings.'

Cathy dabbed her eyes with a crumpled tissue from her pocket. 'Most of the time it's fine, he's nice and I'm quite happy, and we have a light-hearted banter together. Sometimes I even look forward to him coming home, but...'

'Yes?'

'He can be changeable, a bit of a Jekyll and Hyde character. He's so loving and tender one moment, kissing and hugging me, then the next minute he's sort of... well, not happy with me, in a subtle sort of way. Then he's loving again. It's getting me down, and then sometimes I think I'm imagining it and I start to doubt myself, as if there's something wrong with me.'

Holly grimaced. 'Why on earth would he be not happy with you? Is he changeable with Jason as well?'

'No, he's perfect with Jason, the best uncle possible.'

'So what do you do that upsets him?'

'Oh, I don't know, small things, like the other day when I was ironing his shirts he insisted I did them a certain way. It just made me feel a bit stupid really.'

'He could iron his own bloody shirts if he's so

pernickety, damn him.'

'And another thing. Before we were married he was so generous, never wanted me to pay for anything unless I insisted, and I thought he was, well, not short of a bob or two. He said when we were married he'd contribute financially. He's gone back on that, says he wants to save up for starting his own business. He won't help with the bills at all.'

'When's he going to start up this business empire?' asked Holly, hands on hips.

'I don't know; soon, he said. He says that we'll be financially secure when it's up and running.'

'He does, does he?'

'He wants to wait until after Christmas when things have settled down a bit, then he's going to look for a workshop.'

'I have my doubts about this venture of his, you know, I can't imagine he's going to make much money repairing bits of equipment. I hope he's thought it through carefully enough.'

'Oh he has, he wants to expand and hire more staff as soon as he can.'

Holly sighed.

'Look, you haven't come here to listen to me, you need to rest and relax, why don't you sit down,' said Cathy.

'I don't care about that. Let's talk about you.'

'Please, sit down.'

Holly sat.

'Have you thought what you'll do for Christmas? You're more than welcome to come to me, George will be there.'

'Thanks, Holly, I'd love to but Simon wants his mother to come here so I suppose I'll have to do that. Jason likes being at home so I expect it'll be OK.'

Holly breathed deeply, sensing there was more. She

looked piercingly at Cathy. 'That's not all, is it? There's something else, I can tell.'

Cathy put her hand to her heart. 'I'd better see what Jason's doing. I can't hear him playing the mirror game anymore.'

'Now *you* sit down, I'll go.'

Cathy sat on the sofa.

Cathy could hear them talking and milling about and then the sound of the abacus. Shortly afterwards Holly returned and sat next to her.

'He's fine, engrossed in counting, six columns of bricks, all different colours. It's all right, we can talk.'

'Softly,' said Cathy.

'So, what is it, what else? Cathy, tell me.'

Cathy was silent for a few moments, then she took a deep breath and pointed to the doorway. 'He's different now.' She stifled tears. 'In the bedroom.'

'Different?' Holly regarded her closely. 'He used to be a considerate lover, I remember you telling me. Don't say he's changed in that department.'

Cathy nodded.

'I'm sorry; that is upsetting.' She studied Cathy silently for a moment. 'Do you want to talk about it?'

Cathy sniffed.

'This is very difficult for me.'

'I can understand that,' said Holly gently.

'It's embarrassing and I feel ashamed.'

'Talking about it?'

'Yes.'

'Whatever you say is between you and me alone. Lovemaking should be a positive experience for you both; if it's not then something isn't right.'

Cathy sniffed again.

After a short while she said, 'He wants to experiment.'

'Experiment? What, with the bloody mirror?'

'Not that, the curtains are closed, but he wants to do things... I don't like.'

'Things you don't like... '

'Yes, quirky... weird things and a bit rough. When I say I don't like it, he says I'm inhibited and a prude.'

'Damn him! If you don't like it, that should be enough.'

'Then because he found out about Ricardo... I can't explain how, it would take too long. Because of that, one moment he accuses me of being a prude, the next he's implying I'm a slut.' She burst into tears again.

Holly took a tissue from her handbag and forced it into Cathy's hand; she got up and paced around the room. 'Bloody man. He's not making you happy, is he?'

'I must adjust to him. Give us time. He's a good man really. I feel as if I'm failing him, expecting too much.'

Before Holly could reply they heard the front door open, some noises and footsteps in the corridor.

'Uncle Simon!' shouted Jason exuberantly. They heard him running to the front door.

Cathy and Holly looked at each other in silence. Cathy quickly wiped her face, got up and smoothed her pinafore.

'Hi Simon, Holly's here,' said Cathy. They went to meet him. Simon gave Jason a hug.

'Oh, lovely to see you, Holly,' said Simon, avoiding her gaze, 'how are you?'

'Fine thanks, Simon. And yourself?'

'I'm good.'

'I'm counting bricks,' said Jason, looking straight at Simon.

'Great, I'll come and play with you soon,' said Simon warmly.

'Yes, please,' Jason ran back into his room.

Simon walked briskly past Cathy and Holly, went into the kitchen and switched on the kettle. Tentatively, they followed.

'How's business?' asked Holly.

'You know, busy. I'm glad to be home though. It's great seeing Cathy and Jason, keeps me going after a long tiring day. You look lovely in that dress, Cathy, by the way. A sight for sore eyes.'

'Well, I think I should be going now,' said Holly.

'Sure, great to see you again,' said Simon, his cold expression belying the sentiment in his words.

Cathy walked her to the door. 'Oh dear, I think he's had a bad day at work,' she said.

'You need to keep in touch with me,' whispered Holly as she stepped into the stairwell.

Cathy nodded. 'I will.'

CHAPTER 18

Cathy looked up from her book. Simon was standing right in front of her. He had his hands in his pockets and was smiling and looking relaxed.

'Are you enjoying that book I bought you for Christmas?'

'Yes thanks.'

'Sorry to interrupt, but when you've finished that chapter, darling, get your coat, I want to take you out.'

'Where are we going?'

'I want to show you something. Something for our future.'

'That sounds mysterious, a bit dramatic. Aren't you going to tell me what it is?'

'I don't want to spoil the surprise.' Simon was grinning broadly.

Cathy felt a tremor of anxiety. 'All right, I'm game, but we've got to be back before 4.00 o'clock because that's when Deirdre's dropping Jason back from the party.'

'Fine, we should be back by then.'

After defrosting the car they got in and Simon turned on the ignition. She could smell his aftershave even though he was wearing his thick winter jacket. This scent was Brut, his favourite, although she knew he had a few. Her hands were chilled; she dipped into her pockets for her gloves. As they fastened their seatbelts Cathy said, 'Not going to blindfold me then?'

'No, it'll be useful if you know the way there,' Simon said before he realised Cathy was joking. He smiled thinly. 'It's not far.'

They set off. At first Cathy was able to recognise the streets but soon there were so many twists and turns down unfamiliar roads that she felt quite disorientated.

'Where are we going, Simon? I don't recognise it here.'

'We're going to a place just outside Pinner, north of Harrow. It's not far.'

After about twenty minutes, Simon pulled up outside a detached house set back from the road with an overgrown garden at the front enclosed by a low wooden fence. There was an estate agent's FOR SALE sign fastened to one of the gateposts.

'Here we are,' said Simon. 'Let's go and have a look, shall we?'

Cathy stiffened. 'What are we doing here? What is this?'

'Cathy, it's an opportunity, for us.' He opened the car door. 'Come and see.'

Cathy hesitated, took a couple of breaths, and with trepidation slowly got out. Simon swung the gate open and gestured for Cathy to precede him up the garden path to the front door. The door opened and a blond-haired young man in a sharp blue suit, white shirt and red tie stood waiting for them. Inside there was dampness in the air and a stale smell.

'Simon, good to see you again,' the young man said, shaking Simon's hand. 'And you must be Cathy,' he said, turning to her. 'I'm pleased to meet you.' He took her hand and shook it warmly. 'My name is Mark Fletcher of Fletcher and Son. But I'm sure Simon has told you all about us, our office is in Pinner High Street.'

Cathy smiled weakly at him, her thoughts in turmoil. 'Hello,' she said.

'I'm sorry the house is a bit cold, being empty. I'm sure Simon's told you that an old lady lived here; she moved into a nursing home a few months ago so it needs a bit of decoration, but it's a well-built, solid 1930s house. Very sought after.' Mark rubbed his hands. 'Simon, why don't

114

you take Cathy round, as you've seen it before.' Cathy darted a sharp glance at Simon. 'I'll wait in the living room, and I'll be happy to answer any questions you may have after you've been round.'

'Good idea,' said Simon, 'come on, Cathy, let's start in the kitchen.'

'What the hell's going on?' hissed Cathy angrily when they were alone. 'Been here before? Are you planning to buy this house?'

Simon opened one kitchen unit after another, peered inside each one and examined the hinges.

'It's a quality kitchen this, and there's lots of storage.'

'Simon!'

He took a deep breath.

'We can buy it together. You'll see it's a good size. With three bedrooms it's an ideal family home for us all. I can set up my workshop in the garage for starters, get my repair business going. It'll be great, just what we need.'

'*We* need?' Cathy almost spat the words out.

'You know I want to set up in business, working for myself. Having a partner was a disaster for me, I was too trusting. And I hate working for those idiots at Venture's. This is a chance for us – all of us. I can start my business here. You and Jason will be happier; a house is much better for a young boy than a flat. There's a very nice garden at the back.' He looked at her and frowned, then said in an irritated tone, 'Come on, Cathy, we've discussed all this before.'

'We've talked about it, yes. But we hadn't come to any conclusions, made any decisions. And now I find you've been looking at this place without me.' Cathy took a step back and crossed her arms in front of her. 'Have you made an offer on it?'

'No, Cathy, I wanted you to see it. Anyway, let's have a look round, particularly as we're here. See what you think.

It's a bargain at what they're asking for it.'

'What are you going to do? Can you afford to buy it yourself, outright?'

Simon rubbed his hands. After a moment he said, 'No, darling, I will need your help with this.'

'So you want me to sell my flat?'

'Yes, darling, our flat; this is for all of us, a new home.'

Cathy felt a wave of heat charge through her. 'You've sprung this on me. We've only been married a few months. Jason's settled in at his school, I'm happy with the flat; it's near my work, near everything familiar. I'm not ready to move.'

'We're hardly moving to Outer Mongolia. But look, you're missing the point. This is a great opportunity, Cathy. It's an adventure for us, a new start. Come on, I'll show you round. Just have a look anyway.'

She sighed. 'Well, as we're here it won't hurt to look, but that's all.' Cathy could feel her eyes welling with tears; she stifled a sob.

Simon looked at her. 'Come on, darling, don't look sad in front of Mark, it's embarrassing.'

Simon opened the back door and ushered Cathy outside. There was a good-sized overgrown lawn, with flowerbeds bordering it. A small wooden shed at the rear stood against the boundary hedge.

'I'll have to replace the shed, I'll need a much bigger space. But this is what I mean about the workshop. And the garden's great, plenty of room for Jason and me to kick a ball about out here as well. He'll love it; much more convenient than having to traipse off to the park all the time.'

'Look, I'm cold, I want to go back inside.'

'Oh, come on, try to see its potential.'

Cathy led the way back through the kitchen into the hallway.

'Let's go upstairs,' said Simon, leading the way. The stairs led to a landing with four doors off it. He strode to the nearest door and opened it. 'This is the master bedroom,' he said, going inside, beckoning Cathy to follow him. Cathy stood in the doorway for a moment then crossed the room and went to the built-in wardrobe that stretched across the whole extent of the rear wall. She slid open the door, which made a squeaking noise as it moved along its track.

'Needs a bit of oil by the sound of it,' said Simon. 'I'll sort it out.'

'It's a reasonably-sized bedroom, if someone wanted to live here,' she said doubtfully.

'It's a really nice room.'

They moved into the corridor. 'And this would be a great room for Jason,' said Simon, and with a flourish he opened the next door.

Cathy went in; she saw that it looked out over the garden. 'I don't like it, it's a bit dark. At the moment he's got a lovely bright room.'

'It only needs a lick of paint, and it has a great view. Come to the window and have a look.'

'It's all right, I can see from here.'

She turned away. Simon hurried after her.

'Here's the bathroom.'

She glanced briefly at the tacky-looking avocado suite. He opened another door.

'The third bedroom is a bit small really to be a bedroom but there's room for a desk and chair and probably a small filing cabinet as well. I could use it as an office.'

Cathy stopped, hands on her hips, and frowned at him.

'You've got it all worked out, haven't you.'

'Don't be like that, Cathy. I told you, it's all for us.'

'Hmm... '

Downstairs, he led her into the living room. Mark stood

quietly in a corner, looking at some papers on a clipboard.

'This is a really bright, spacious room, don't you think, Cathy?' She looked around; there was a fireplace on one side and a bay window at the front. 'And here's the dining room.' He led her into the back room overlooking the garden. 'There's plenty of room here for all our furniture.' He sighed. 'I think this house is great, it's just what we need.'

'Well, how do you like the house?' asked Mark, coming towards them.

'It's even better than I remembered. Cathy likes it as well, don't you, Cathy?'

Cathy crossed her arms. 'I haven't had time to think about it yet, but it's not bad, as houses go.'

'That's high praise, coming from her,' said Simon, winking at Mark.

'Do you have any questions, either of you?' He looked at each in turn, but they shook their heads.

'Well, Simon, do you think you will make an offer?'

'We need to talk it over.'

'Of course. I'll wait to hear from you. Nice to have met you, Cathy,' Mark said, shaking her hand. 'And nice to see you again, Simon.'

Driving back to the flat, there was a strained silence in the car.

CHAPTER 19

Simon, grunting, walked straight into the kitchen, loosened his tie, flopped down into the wicker chair with his legs splayed and heaved a sigh.

'Oh dear, not a good day then.' Cathy stiffened.

'Bloody awful week.'

'Why is that?'

'I've been driving for hours. Swindon, Northampton, up to Durham. It was snowing, really held me up. Then down to Norwich.' With a quick thrust of his hand he undid and pulled off his tie. 'I got there later than expected, couldn't be bothered to drive back last night. You weren't waiting up for me, I hope.'

She began emptying the washing machine, glancing at him every now and then between taking the wet clothes out and arranging them on the clothes-horse.

'No, you said you might get caught away; it's all right.'

'I didn't have time to phone.'

'I expected that.'

'I've criss-crossed the whole country dealing with awkward customers, smiling and buttering them up with compliments even though I think they're pricks. The one I saw today, Brecon and Sons, millionaires they are, but they can't make a decision until the end of March when they've got their new budgets. Bastards.' There was bitterness in his tone.

'Where did you stay?'

'In Ipswich, at *The Red Lion.*'

'I see.'

He leant back, his arms above his head. 'I'm not sure how much longer I can go on like this, it's wearing me down.'

'Can I get you a coffee or something?'

His tone softened. 'Oh, thanks, that would be nice.' He smiled gently at her, quietly considering for a moment. 'Have you had any more thoughts about the house in Broomfield Way, the one we went to see together a couple of weeks ago, remember? I've been thinking about it while I've been driving around, about what a good buy it is.'

She turned and switched on the kettle.

'Come and sit down, darling,' he said.

She slowly crossed the kitchen, swung the aluminium chair round, placed it at right angles to him and sat down.

'I'm exhausted myself.'

He studied her for a moment.

'So, but what about the house?'

She twisted away. 'Oh, that. I haven't really given it much thought. I've been busy moving a backlog of paperwork. I've wanted to do it for months.'

His face dropped.

'Oh, come on, darling.' There was frustration in his voice. 'It's such a great opportunity.'

Cathy looked towards the window.

'You can see how miserable I am in my job.' His tone softened again. 'Just imagine us in our own house. Me working from home; seeing so much more of you both. I want to spend more time with you and Jason.'

Cathy leant her elbow on the table, rested her cheek on her hand and glanced at him briefly. The kettle boiled and she got up. While she was making the coffee she heard him tapping his fingers on the table. She put the cup in front of him and sat down again.

'Thanks,' he said. He leant forward. 'I spoke to Jason about it... about how, if we were living in a house, he could play outside whenever he wanted. He said he'd like a garden.'

Cathy frowned. 'Why did you do that? It's not your

place to put ideas in his head, especially when we haven't decided anything.'

Simon tilted his head back and looked at the ceiling.

'OK, maybe I was jumping the gun a bit, but you need to think about it. It's a really good buy.'

'No, Simon, I'm really not ready. I'm sorry you're not happy in your work, but the time doesn't feel right. Please can we drop the subject.'

She got up and finished emptying the washing machine.

He looked at his watch. 'Anyway, at least I'm back in time to take Jason to football this evening. I broke every speed limit to get here the last few miles. I didn't want to let him down.' He looked around. 'By the way, where is he?'

She bit her lip, slowly straightened up, closed the washing machine door with a soft click and turned to face him. 'He's gone for a sleepover with his friend Billy for the weekend.'

'You changed our arrangement? You knew we were going to the match?' he hissed, scowling.

She retreated into a corner of the kitchen. 'I hadn't heard from you.'

'I bust a gut trying to get back in time and you go and make another arrangement. He was looking forward to going to the match with me.'

'He won't miss it; he's going with Billy and his dad.'

'Bloody wonderful,' he spluttered. 'What about me?'

'What about you? This was for Jason. OK, you like it, but it's not for you. Besides, I had no idea when you'd be back.'

'You wanted him to have a Dad, remember!'

Cathy felt her heart pound and hesitated for a moment. 'But not at any cost,' she whispered under her breath.

He eyed her furiously.

'What do you want? I'm here, aren't I, being a Dad to

Jason, fixing your light bulbs, earning money, creating the ideal little family you wanted, planning a good future for us all... and you go and sabotage it, you silly bitch.'

Cathy felt a flush of heat on her cheeks; she put her hands to her face, her eyes welling with tears.

He sat there for a few moments, studying her dispassionately. Suddenly he got up, went to her and embraced her tenderly. 'Oh, darling, I've upset you.' Rocking her in his arms, he sounded genuinely remorseful. 'I shouldn't have said those things, it's not what I really feel, I love you so much... I'm just tired, I'm sorry.' Cathy felt him supporting her, his arms warm and comforting, and despite her heightened emotions, she relaxed. 'It's been really hard for you on your own all these years, hasn't it? You've struggled and I know you're scared of the future, but you need to trust me now.' He kissed her tenderly on her cheek and stroked her hair. 'Look at me, Cathy. Are you OK?'

She looked up at him.

'Yes.'

'I'm sorry; let me make it up to you. Let me think.' He rocked her for a moment longer. 'Do you want to go out for dinner now Jason's away?'

'No, I'm really not in the mood.'

He rocked her again and hummed something she didn't recognise.

'Well, I think I'd like to go to *The Rose and Crown* for a drink, to unwind instead. Is that OK with you?'

'Sure. I'd like a little time on my own I think,' she said, sniffling.

He took her hand and led her to the front door.

'Keep the bed warm,' he said as he left, and Cathy shivered.

* * *

Two hours later Simon stumbled through the front door. His face was red and he smelt of liquor and something else unpleasant: cigarette smoke, sweat?

'Where's my wife?' he said gruffly, slurring his words.

'Oh dear! You look terrible and you smell worse.' She heard the tremor in her own voice.

'Come on,' he pulled her towards the bedroom. 'I want to see my wife in the mirror, see what she's like when she's really relaxed.'

'Simon, how much have you drunk? You need to lie down, sleep it off.'

'Good, you're ready, are you? Do you know who I am or don't you care?' He threw off his shoes. 'Plumber, window cleaner, candlestick-maker, anyone will do. Come on, you little tart; open your legs for me.'

'You're drunk,' said Cathy sharply, her heart pounding.

'You need to be shown how to behave, Mrs. To obey your husband.'

He tried to pull her onto the bed. She resisted, kicking and shoving him away.

'Simon, stop it!'

'My dick wants servicing.'

She pulled free. Simon threw off his coat, unzipped his fly and flopped back on to the bed, a dead weight. A few moments later he was snoring heavily.

CHAPTER 20

'Hello, Holly, come in' said Cathy sheepishly, stepping aside.

Holly noticed Cathy's shoulders were slumped and she moved stiffly, avoiding her gaze. Holly clicked the front door shut behind her.

'Are you OK?' Holly scanned her. 'Another new dress, but what's with the scarf round your neck? And the dark glasses?'

'Oh, nothing, I've got a rash. It's a bit ugly. I've put cream on it, it will be fine,' said Cathy dismissively. 'I just didn't want you to see these ugly spots, that's all.'

Holly's eyes narrowed. 'And the dark glasses? In February?'

Cathy cleared her throat. 'I've got some problem with my eye, conjunctivitis I think. My eyes are a bit itchy and light-sensitive; that's the problem, no matter.' She shrugged her shoulders.

'Don't you think you should see a doctor?'

'No, I don't want to bother with that,' said Cathy cheerily.

'Have you had this before?'

'No... well I might have, some time ago. With the cream on it, the rash will go quickly I expect. Don't make a fuss, Holly.'

'Let me look at it.'

'No!' shouted Cathy, taking two steps backwards. 'Sorry, didn't mean to shout. Honestly, I'm fine.' She smoothed her belted green corduroy dress. 'Now, coffee?' she said in a friendlier tone.

Holly looked askance at Cathy but decided not to push her further.

'Yes please, darling.'

Cathy went to the kitchen and Holly took off her shoes then settled herself on the sofa in the living room. Cathy came in with two drinks, passed Holly her cup and saucer and sat down in the armchair.

'I've bought an Easter egg for Jason,' said Holly, passing it to Cathy. 'It's early this year, in March.'

'Oh, thank you, that's really nice.'

'It's his sixth birthday as well soon, isn't it. The second of April.'

'Yes, well remembered.'

'I thought I'd buy him a scooter. I saw one in a shop window I thought would fit him perfectly. What do you think?'

'I think he'd like that.'

'I'll drop it round sometime.'

'That would be great. Thanks.' They sipped their coffees. 'How's work,' asked Cathy, 'still working you to the bone?'

'Yes, as busy as ever. I need to go to Barcelona next month, check on the new store. It's doing OK. I may have to do more travelling than usual, not that I really want to.'

'The company's doing well then, it always seems to be, it must be because of you.'

'It's a team effort. But I can't complain.'

'My life seems very limited and routine compared with yours.' Cathy sat stiffly, picking her nails, her legs propped underneath her.

'You have darling Jason to look after. A vital job. Me, I'm just earning a living.'

Cathy shrugged and there was a strained silence.

'So how have things been? Simon? Is he still... moody?'

'He's fine... well, that's not completely right, he can be a bit grumpy sometimes, but that's when he's tired. He works very long hours, you know.'

'I see.' They sat in silence again for a few moments. 'Does he still have time for Jason?'

'When they are together Simon's brilliant; when he's home early enough he always reads to him, he's so devoted.'

Holly had the saucer in one hand, cup in the other. She took a sip of her coffee, then, taking her time, placed the cup back on its saucer, put it down on the table, and regarded Cathy searchingly.

'Cathy,' she said, 'we've been friends for years and years. Don't try to fool me. You haven't got a rash at all, have you?'

'What sort of stupid question is that, of course I have!'

Holly noticed her tremble suddenly. Cathy got up, turned away and burst out crying.

'The rotten bastard.' Holly stood up abruptly. 'The sleazy git, I'll kill him. Let me see, show me what he's done to you.'

She stood right in front of Cathy.

'No... please... ' Cathy blustered, putting her hands protectively in front of her face.

'Yes, you must, because I care,' said Holly, decisively but gently pulling Cathy's arms down towards her side.

'OK... OK.'

Cathy removed the glasses and placed them on the arm of the sofa. As she raised her face Holly gasped. Her left eye was almost swollen shut, with a dark black bruise already showing above her brow. The other was red-sore from crying.

'Shit! Hanging's too good for him,' spat Holly. 'Show me the rest.'

'What rest?'

'Your neck of course.'

Sniffing, Cathy unwound the scarf from around her

neck; the left side was black with a deep scratch.

'Was that his nails?'

Cathy nodded.

'Poor love,' said Holly with feeling.

'It's not wholly his fault,' she said. 'It's partly mine as well.'

'He knocks you about... and you... you say it's not his fault! Of course it's his fault, it's all his bloody fault. Come on, Cathy, get real!'

'He wants me to sell the flat so we can buy a house, a house with a workshop in the garden so he can start his business.'

'And you don't want to.'

'No... he got cross.'

'Now *I'm* cross, bloody furious in fact. There's never any justification for hitting you, never.' Holly's chest heaved.

'Well, there is, you see.'

'You're talking rot, Cathy. I can't believe you just said that.'

'There's something else, something more serious.'

'Oh my God, what else has he done?'

'No, he hasn't done anything else; it's a deeper problem, in our relationship.'

'That's bloody obvious but the problem is not you, it's him.'

'I don't love him, you see, and he knows it.'

'I'm not surprised if he thumps you. He doesn't deserve your affection!'

'No, no, before that. It was all a mistake, I made a terrible mistake. I can't love anyone else you see.'

'Anyone else? What do you mean?'

Cathy turned away momentarily, then twisting to face Holly, grabbed the back of the sofa, breathing heavily.

'I'm still in love with Jason's father. Isn't it obvious?

Sometimes you can be so slow, Holly.'

Holly stood still for a moment, her eyes focused on Cathy, considering.

'Whether you love him or not, that's no excuse for thumping you. He's just a bastard and probably always was. What a bloody mess this is. Look, I don't want to be cruel, but leaving Simon aside, you have to let go of the past, you have to move on... Jason's father's dead, and he's not coming back. You can't let it hold you back, you have to take control and get on with your life.'

'I've tried so hard, Holly, so hard.' She sniffed. 'I used to write him these letters, many of them, letters I would never send.'

'Letters... to Jason's father?'

'Yes.'

'But... that's quite bizarre, Cathy.' Holly shook her head. 'I can't say I can understand how it must feel to have lost the father of your new baby but... what for? What can be achieved?'

'Don't look at me like that, Holly.'

'Like what?'

'So questioning.'

'I'm sorry, darling, I'm just trying to understand. Please go on.'

Cathy swallowed hard.

'Then I got all these letters, they were in a bundle, and... and... I had this ritual. I burnt them all in a fire on the grassy verge, near the canal, and threw the ashes into the water. I did it when I met Simon. I thought I would forget him after that, it was supposed to be healing.'

'You loved him very much. I suspected all along that you never really got over him. But you have to put him behind you now for Jason's sake.'

Cathy paced around, gesticulating. 'And this is the most terrible thing. You remember the headmistress called me

128

in?'

'Yes.'

'Well, it was because Jason was talking about his father coming back, they were worried about him, and I'm to blame, it's because I was never really clear with Jason.' She put her hands on her cheeks. 'I hadn't told him explicitly that his father was dead. Well, after that I had to, so I told him outright, just like that. "Your father is dead," I said to him. What a terrible, terrible thing to say.'

Cathy burst into tears and wailed loudly, bent over with emotion.

'That was the right thing to do.'

'It was after that that I burnt the letters,' she said between sobs. 'I thought it was for the best, would bring closure, allow me to move on, to make space for Simon to come into my life and for Jason to be ready for a new Dad.'

'And it hasn't?'

Cathy stood stock-still, with the scarf in both hands pressed tightly to her heaving chest. She looked at Holly with tormented, flashing eyes and slowly shook her head from side to side. Tears trickled down her red, flushed cheeks.

'Cathy, darling, what is it?'

'I need to tell you something.'

'About Jason's father?'

'Yes,' she whispered.

'What about him?'

Cathy breathed deeply, her chest heaving. They were silent for a few moments, Cathy's piercing look becoming more intense every moment. It seemed to burn into Holly's consciousness. Something strange seemed to pass between them, an understanding.

'He's not dead?' asked Holly softly, wide-eyed.

'He may not be dead,' Cathy whispered.

'Not dead.' Holly nodded slowly. They looked at each other in silence for a long time. 'Then where is he?'

Cathy gulped. 'I'm not sure.'

'You… don't know?' She frowned and stared fixedly at Cathy, trying to read the message in the passionate intensity of her friend's gaze.

'I have an idea where he might be.'

'Well… is he with someone else? Is that it?'

'No… but he's lost to me. He's locked away.'

'What… in prison?'

'No, but he might as well be, seeing where he is.'

'Hospital? Nursing home, lunatic asylum? Has he been in a terrible accident? Is he in a coma? You poor thing, Cathy, you've lost your lover… and Jason's lost his natural father.'

Cathy paced up and down. 'No, no, you've got it all wrong. He's not ill or incapacitated,' Cathy's voice cracked, 'I'm sure he would be with us… if he knew, but he doesn't.'

'Doesn't know? Doesn't know what?'

'About Jason… He doesn't know he's a father. He doesn't know we have a son!'

'Why the hell not?' shouted Holly, shaking her head. 'Why in God's name didn't you tell him?'

'Because... he's doing something very important… important to him.'

'What is he doing that's more important than looking after his family… helping to bring up his son?'

Cathy burst into tears again, stood quietly for a few moments, then shook her head and took a few deep breaths, her face bright red, her chest heaving.

'Tell me, for goodness' sake!'

They were silent for a few moments, the atmosphere tight with frizzling emotion.

Cathy took another deep breath.

'OK... OK... he's a...' she looked Holly in the eye. 'He's a monk!'

Holly's eyes widened. 'He's a what?'

'A monk.'

'A monk... ' repeated Holly incredulously and blinked a few times. 'Well, that does take the biscuit. A monk... What sort of monk?'

'Buddhist of course, you know, shaven head, saffron robes,' said Cathy impatiently.

'You had a passionate affair with a Buddhist monk?' Holly's voice was slow and quiet, as if she didn't quite believe it.

'He hadn't taken his vows at the time.'

'A Buddhist monk... my God, this is a surprise.' Holly took a few deep breaths, her hand over her mouth. 'I need to take this in.' She paced up and down the room. 'It's a shock... a big shock.' She looked straight at Cathy. 'I think I'd have been less surprised if you'd told me he was a serial bigamist or a criminal mastermind or something.' Holly and Cathy stared at each other in silence. Then Cathy giggled. Holly started to giggle as well, and the giggles built up as they examined each other, then became laughter. Then they both roared with laughter, which went on and on until they were doubled up and Holly fell into the sofa clutching her stomach. Cathy collapsed in the armchair in fits, tears streaming down her face. For a full five minutes they couldn't stop.

'This is the pits for my mascara, darling, do you have a tissue?' said Holly eventually.

Cathy pulled a small packet out of her pocket, wiped her own eyes with one tissue then threw the packet to Holly. Holly dabbed her eyes.

'I haven't laughed so long since... I can't remember when,' Holly said.

'Nor me... No, yes I can. Do you remember when we

were drunk in that pub in Swindon. Girls' weekend away…
We were about eighteen.'

'Yes, I do.'

'There were these blokes we fancied at the other side of
the bar. And the ugly one tried to chat us up.'

'Vaguely… Anyway, good to laugh with you, darling.
Like old carefree times. So… ' she said between giggles,
'where is he, your Buddhist monk?'

'He's meditating.'

'Of course he is, and where might that be?'

'Somewhere in Vietnam, a monastery… I don't know
exactly where.'

'Vietnam… that's a hell of a long way away. Not
surprised you can't keep track of him. So, this monk of
yours, how did you meet him? Not in Vietnam?'

'No, at work, he wasn't a monk then.'

'No, I expect not... Look, darling, I really need a drink,
a stiff whisky. That Scotch I bought you for Christmas;
there's some left I hope.'

Cathy went to the kitchen, fetched the bottle and poured
whiskies for them both.

'Anything with it?' asked Cathy as she poured the
liquor into two crystal glasses.

'No, neat, I need it neat.'

Cathy passed her the glass.

'Crystal. I haven't seen those before.'

'They're Simon's.'

They both downed the whisky in one.

'More,' said Holly.

Cathy refilled their glasses and sat down in the
armchair.

Holly settled herself comfortably on the sofa; an
intrigued expression crept over her face.

'So… this is completely extraordinary, where exactly
did you meet him?'

'We both worked for a company called BCS, in the research department. You might remember I was a research assistant when you were in California.'

'Yes, I do.'

'He was my manager.'

'What was his background?'

'He went to Cambridge, a degree in Physics... He headed up the department... There were about ten of us.'

'Not easy for either of you, I imagine?'

'No... it was so drawn out, over a really long period, months. So many times he hinted that he liked me... then he'd withdraw or go away on conferences. For so long it was agony, I never knew where I was with him. Then, when we got together, he told me he'd loved me all the time.'

'So why did he hesitate?'

'Apart from work he was living quietly... like a monk, you see... when he wasn't at work.'

'What a fascinating love story. Why didn't you tell him you were pregnant?'

'I wasn't sure I was pregnant, and the time was never right.' Cathy sighed. 'Anyway, he'd committed to going back. I thought if I told him I might be pregnant he'd stay for me and our child... but at the time he wanted to go back.'

'You've shown unbelievable self-sacrifice... in fact on the level of the ridiculous. Back? You mean he'd been there before?'

'Yes, he lived in the monastery before; the monks... they were hiding him.'

'When? From what?'

Cathy got up and paced the room.

'It was during the Vietnam War, he was in Vietnam working with the British Government against the Viet Cong. He was recruited from Cambridge, you see... His

133

work was dangerous, he had to escape and was very lucky… the monks took him under their protection into their monastery. Then, after a few years, he was ordained himself.' Cathy frowned. 'Look, please don't ask me any more questions, I've told you too much already… I really shouldn't have,' she whispered.

Holly took a deep breath and a gulp of whisky.

'I didn't follow the Vietnam War very closely but I thought Britain stayed out of it.'

Cathy sat down again, perched on the edge of the armchair.

'Apparently not … officially we were just training the Americans, but there were other things going on. It was all very hush-hush.'

'So what was his job?'

'He was a translator in the Embassy… he spoke fluent Vietnamese and French. He lived in the Far East as a child.'

'But that wasn't all he was doing?'

'No.'

'Was he a spy?'

'Look, stop asking me these questions. It's enough, honestly.'

'So you believe your Buddhist monk, the things he's told you?'

'Of course I fucking believe him, how stupid of you! Stop! Enough, I've told you enough.' She put her hands over her ears. 'You're so suspicious! First Simon, now Jason's father. Don't you trust anyone?'

Holly took another deep breath.

'Let's change the subject, tell me about George,' said Cathy calmly.

Holly went quiet for a while, gathering her thoughts.

'OK… George got some time off at last, we stole away for a weekend in Oxford, in an intimate little hotel, four-poster bed, cottagey garden, the works. It was all very quaint and restful. Now he's in Dubai, then Abu Dhabi, next Bahrain... I shan't see him again until Friday week, at the earliest. It does seem a long time sometimes.'

'Must be... to be separated from the one you love,' said Cathy pensively.

'But I'm not like you in that way, you know. I never wanted a home or family, in fact I'm happiest travelling and living out of a suitcase. So is George. But you... you're different. I always wanted to see you and Jason settled. I thought that this time you might be... what a bloody mess.'

'That sort of happiness is a fantasy; it is for me anyway.'

'I didn't say happy all the time... I said settled.'

Cathy got up again and stood by the window, looking out.

'But you're clearly not,' said Holly.

'How can I be? Simon has been at best a disappointment, at worst a disaster. It started so well.'

'And I feel responsible.'

'You're not, Holly. I made all my own choices. You were just trying to help me.'

They were silent for a few moments.

'What's his name?'

'Whose name?'

'Jason's father.'

'Annando.'

'No, silly, his real name.'

'He probably thinks that is his "real" name now.'

'You know what I mean, his English name... You've never told me.'

Cathy turned and faced Holly.

'Does it matter? He's on the other side of the world. You'll never meet him.'

'I suppose it doesn't matter… but I just want to know a little more about him. It sounds strange thinking of you having a son with "Annando" but it doesn't seem so strange to think of you with "John Smith".'

'If you must... it's Blake.'

'Blake what?'

'What about him?' she said dismissively.

'His surname?'

Cathy sighed. 'Carter.'

'I see... nice name.'

Hmm, Blake Carter: that's a strong-sounding name, and quite unusual, mused Holly, and her mind started to work overtime.

CHAPTER 21

Animated conversation and soft music emanated from the open window as Holly and George approached the smart Georgian house in the deepening twilight. Holly's stilettos made sharp clicks on the stone steps as she climbed to the front door. She felt the cool evening breeze through her chiffon gown. The front doorbell made a soft chime.

'Welcome, come in.' Freda embraced them both warmly and ushered them in. Her long turquoise blue evening gown trailed on the floor.

In the elegant hallway Holly smelt the scent of fresh flowers; daffodils and irises had been carefully arranged in a Chinese vase.

'So good to see you after so long,' continued Freda. 'You look wonderful, darling, wonderful. Robin is entertaining our old friends Audrey and Vincent. Come and meet them.'

In the vastness of the living room the furniture looked as if it would not be out of place in an expensive auction house. The curtains were red velvet and the sofas were enhanced with colourful silk cushions. Elaborate crystal chandeliers hung from the ceiling, bathing the room in a mellow warm glow.

After the usual pleasantries, drinks and small talk, they were summoned through to the dining room.

'Freda is such a wonderful cook,' said Audrey in a light sing-song voice, her manner slightly fey. 'I love coming here. Her salmon au gratin is the very best in West Hampstead. Don't you agree, Holly?'

'Absolutely. I'm not going to waste this opportunity to have some decent cordon bleu.'

'Do you cook yourself?' asked Audrey.

'Not much, to be honest.'

'Oh, really, don't you enjoy it?'

'I work away from home most of the time so I eat out, hotels mainly. I've never tried anything as good as Freda's home cooking of course.'

'Thank you, Holly, I do enjoy cooking,' said Freda, 'and you're always so complimentary!'

They settled down around the dining table laid with a crisp linen tablecloth. There were two large wooden bowls, both full of salad with diced yellow and red peppers mingled with cherry tomatoes on a mixture of red and green lettuces. 'Looks marvellous,' said Audrey.

Arranged in a circle were several small silver dishes, variously containing shredded carrot, diced beetroot and short strips of coconut.

After the appetizer and small talk where Robin dominated the conversation with his favourite subjects, the Hampstead rugby club and the highs and lows of the stock exchange, and Freda's eyes started glazing over with boredom, the conversation took a new tack.

'So what is your favourite dish, when you're in your different hotels?' asked Freda, looking over at Holly.

'Hmm, I'm rather partial to risotto.'

'Oh, rice!' said Vincent. 'Rice was about the only thing we ate when we were in Vietnam and Cambodia. Do you remember, Audrey?'

Holly's ears pricked up.

'Of course, we've only been back a couple of months. We were there the first two weeks of January. Vincent insisted on buying from the street vendors; it was ladled straight out of the giant pots into bamboo bowls. I was always worried he'd get ill. It all looked very unhygienic.'

'It was the smell, of course. Irresistible, and quite delicious.' Vincent smacked his lips.

'I'll bring the main dish through,' said Freda. 'Robin,

will you pour everyone some wine. I hope you're all OK with red.'

Robin was pouring the last of the wine into his own glass when Freda came back into the room. She set down a large ceramic casserole dish on a wooden mat in the centre of the table. When Freda lifted the lid, the room filled with the aroma of cinnamon and garlic.

'It smells delicious, this is wonderful', said Holly. 'What is it?'

'It's a recipe I brought back from our trip to Morocco when we were last there,' said Freda.

In turn, they helped themselves to the food.

Holly turned to Vincent. 'Talking of trips, what was it like in Vietnam?'

'It's exotic and underdeveloped; they're not really geared up for tourists, which is a bonus we thought. You can see the country untainted, so to speak,' said Vincent.

'Do tell me about it, I have a friend who has a contact there.' Holly smiled encouragingly at him.

'Holly has a sudden fascination with all things Vietnamese. I think I'll have to take her there soon, though goodness knows when we'll find the time,' said George.

'How you exaggerate,' said Holly dismissively. 'Just a passing interest, that's all.'

'What would you like to know?' asked Vincent enthusiastically, looking straight at her.

Holly sat back for a moment. How shall I approach this, she thought.

'The culture, what did you see, any interesting buildings?'

Vincent took a swig of his red wine.

'Now, let me see. Well, you'd be very surprised but the heart of Ho Chi Ming city, which used to be old Saigon, is called the Paris of the Orient. There are these classical buildings and French villas, just as impressive as Paris; you don't feel as if you're in Asia at all.'

'Really?' said Holly.

'But the goods on sale are all Asian, no branded goods or chains of shops that you get in European cities at all.' Audrey spun the stem of her glass between her fingers. 'I loved browsing. They had these bamboo knick-knacks – little bowls and boats – and tiny ceramic figurines, colourful silk fabrics. It was like a treasure trove. Shopping was such a delight!'

'Yes, we did spend a lot of time in shops, rather more than I would have liked,' Vincent grimaced, 'but they were intriguing.'

'What about the local culture. Any Buddhist temples?' asked Holly.

'We did see a lot on tour, they all seemed quite ancient,' said Audrey, unrolling her embroidered napkin from its silver napkin ring and draping it over her lap.

'In fact we did get rather bored seeing so many temples, didn't we?'

'Yes, we did.'

'Any monasteries?'

Vincent sat back and ruminated.

'A couple; and I remember there was one which was particularly interesting. After we took the three-day trip up the Mekong into the heart of rural Vietnam, paddy fields everywhere. Somewhere near Delat. Do you remember, Audrey?'

'Yes, I do. Something rather unusual was going on there. Some of the monks spoke English.'

Holly choked on her cherry tomato. They all looked at her.

'Are you all right?' asked Freda.

'Yes, perfectly,' said Holly. 'Do go on.' She dabbed her mouth with the napkin.

'We wouldn't have been so surprised if it was French,

as Vietnam was once a French colony.'

'English,' said Robin. 'That's hard to believe. How on earth?'

'Yes, we were incredulous as well, weren't we, at first,' said Vincent. 'It was such a remote, isolated place.'

'But who would teach the monks English, and why?' enquired Freda.

'There was this story we were told about an enigmatic English monk, quite senior, who spoke fluent Vietnamese as well as several other European languages; apparently it was he who was teaching the monks English,' said Vincent. 'He was very popular amongst the locals and had a sizeable following.'

Holly put her knife and fork down and sat up straight. 'What was his name, this monk?'

'Oh, I can't remember, can you, Vincent? said Audrey.

Vincent shrugged.

'Something beginning with A?' He looked into the distance. 'Andrew? No, it would be an oriental-type Buddhist name. It escapes me. I can't remember.'

'It doesn't matter, I was just curious,' said Holly. 'Did you meet him?'

'No, from what I remember, he was in seclusion, on retreat. The tour guide had met him. When she spoke about him she was very animated,' said Audrey.

'Well,' said George. 'An English monk is a bit of a curiosity I expect.'

'They probably all want to learn English from the respectable English renunciate,' said Robin. 'Strange that he's a Buddhist monk, though. It's not even his culture.'

'Yes, it is unusual,' mused Freda.

'So, what was it called, this monastery?' asked Holly. 'The one with the English monk.'

'I really can't remember,' said Audrey, looking vacant, 'it has an impossible to pronounce oriental name. Can you

141

remember, Vincent?'

'Not a chance.'

'Does it really matter?' asked George, studying Holly quizzically.

'No, of course not... It doesn't matter at all.' Holly looked into the distance, and as ideas came to her she began to hatch her plan.

CHAPTER 22

Holly's head buzzed, her thoughts whirling. She sighed, closed her eyes and leaned back on the chair. Behind her she heard the rustle of papers and the click of a briefcase being shut; someone got up, the chair was pushed aside and there were soft footsteps on the carpet fading into the distance. Holly opened her eyes. She liked the atmosphere of Hampstead Library, it was quiet and academic and there was a faint smell of furniture polish and old books. Tall wooden bookcases full of hardbacks with dark leather spines stood sedately all around her, reminding her of college days, when she did her MSc at the London Business School. Her mind wandered; it was in the LBS library that she had first set eyes on George. He had been sitting quietly in a corner, looking studious. His thick dark hair reached down to his shoulders, round spectacles were perched on his nose. When he looked up and smiled she was smitten. She focused again. The soft yellow glow of the desk lamp illuminated the papers, books and catalogues strewn on the desk in front of her. Numerous bookmarks stuck out between the pages. She now had a list of forty-eight monasteries in Vietnam. Would it be enough? The information from the library lists had been substantial, but a lot of it was years old and probably out of date. She remembered the indifferent young girl with slanting eyes from the Vietnamese Embassy telling her they didn't provide that kind of information to members of the general public. When Holly had courteously asked to see the Manager, as this was a matter of importance, the girl had reluctantly picked up the phone, had a brief, incomprehensible conversation with unknown persons, curtly said 'No, Madam' and promptly shown her the door.

All Holly's considerable powers of persuasion, which usually yielded results, were useless there. The inscrutable girl had been an impenetrable wall.

A Thai assistant, Lek, at Holly's company had suggested writing to the monasteries directly. Holly decided to concentrate on the ones around the area of Delat. Lek had warned her that the post was unreliable and slow. Holly had been cagey about the purpose of her enquiry, of course; keeping things quiet when necessary was a skill she had learnt after years in business. There were few people she trusted. I'm not going to give up until I've tracked down the mysterious Blake Carter, whether he was the English monk Audrey and Vincent were speaking of or not, she thought. Although all this effort might have seemed altruistic, she knew her motives weren't completely unselfish. She was intrigued to know what he was like. Of course, finding him might go badly wrong for him and Cathy but it was a risk she felt she had to take. She turned over a page in the directory. There was a colour photograph of a Buddhist monk. The caption read 'Venerable Succichitto'. His features were distinctively oriental, his head was shaven and he was dressed in saffron robes. She studied the picture for a long time.

A young man sat down at a nearby desk opposite her. After carefully removing his jacket and placing it on the back of the chair, he opened a leather box and took out a silver fountain pen, then some papers from a folder. Briefly he glanced at Holly, who dropped her gaze, but not before seeing that he had startlingly blue eyes. She wondered what Blake would look like: western in appearance but with a shaven head and traditional robes? Cathy had not described him but if he was anything like Jason he would be quite good-looking. Come on, get on with it, she said to herself and put pen to paper. 'Venerable Annando... ' she began. I can't go too wrong addressing him like this, she thought, they all seem to be called Venerable something or other... She began scribbling:

March 27th 1987

3 Laburnum Walk,
Hampstead,
West London,
UK

Dear Venerable Annando,
Thank you for reading this letter. I am hoping that you are the Venerable Annando I am searching for. This Venerable Annando is English and also has an English name: Blake Carter. If you are not Blake Carter then please forgive me for disturbing your peace. If you are Blake Carter then again I apologise for disturbing you and would not have done so if I didn't believe contacting you was essential. I am a friend of Cathy Simpson but she doesn't know that I am writing to you and would reprimand me if she did. My dear friend Cathy is in some difficulty at the moment and I think that you may be in a unique position to help her. For reasons of confidentiality I will not describe her situation in this letter in any more detail than I have given here. I have been told the post is poor in Vietnam. In case of a very long delay between my posting and you receiving this letter I enclose at the end of this letter her address at the time of writing.
Many thanks
Holly Lansdowne
PS. Of course, if you answer my letter I can tell you more. My address is above.

Holly added Cathy's address, put down her pen and

sighed. There was just enough information to make him interested but not too much if the letter got into the wrong hands. It would have to do. She wrote it again on a new piece of paper in her clearest handwriting, went to the photocopier, made 48 copies, and signed each one.

CHAPTER 23

'Thanks for coming,' said Cathy loudly, above the noise of children milling about at the front door.

There were whoops of laughter as the parents helped the children on with their coats and shoes.

'We've had a lovely time, haven't we, Billy? Say thank you,' said Billy's mother.

'Thank you,' said the little boy, grasping his party bag.

Cathy opened the door and the guests spilled out into the hallway and down the stairs.

Exhausted but happy, Cathy went back to the kitchen where Simon and Margaret sat round the table with Jason; he was kneeling on a chair with a pile of presents in front of him.

'Can I open them now, Mummy?' he asked, his face beaming with excitement.

'Yes, go on.' Cathy took a seat.

'Aren't you pleased I made you wait, Jason? Now we can really concentrate on your presents without all your noisy friends here,' said Simon cheerfully.

Jason grabbed the biggest, a huge box covered in colourful birthday paper with *Age 6* printed on it.

'No, no, darling, I want you to open mine first,' said Margaret, passing him a present scrappily wrapped in tissue paper.

Jason looked at Cathy, who nodded. Simon pulled the huge box away from Jason.

Margaret simpered, 'I do hope you like it.'

Jason whipped off the paper and pulled out a small soft toy rabbit in pale blue with long stiff ears and small beady eyes. From her position Cathy could see that a seam was

147

unravelling and the stuffing was bulging through the split.

'Oh,' Jason said, looked at it for a moment, put it to one side, and looked excitedly at the other presents.

'Say thank you, Jason,' said Cathy.

'Thank you, Grandma Margaret,' said Jason, looking up at her briefly.

'It's a pleasure, Jason. I hope you have many happy hours with it.'

That's a strange present, thought Cathy. The only soft toy he's ever been interested in is Snowy; she must know that, and this must be cheap if it's falling apart so soon. What a shame.

'May I see it please, Jason,' said Margaret.

Jason grabbed hold of the toy rabbit by its ear and tossed it to her. 'Here, Grandma.'

Just as I thought, he doesn't like it much, thought Cathy.

'I'll put a small stitch in it,' whispered Margaret in Cathy's ear as she examined the toy. 'He won't notice.'

Jason grabbed another present. Cathy read the label. 'This is from Edward,' she said.

He unwrapped a lift-the-flap book about trains. The next present was also a book, *The Tiger Who Came to Tea*. Jason eagerly flicked through the pages. They watched as he opened more presents from his friends.

'Such a lovely party,' said Margaret. 'I thought you said you didn't cook, but that was a splendid cake you made, and quite delicious.'

'Well, I did try my best for a special sixth birthday,' said Cathy. 'Glad you liked it.'

Jason picked another present.

'This one's from me,' said Cathy.

He opened a large box of Lego bricks with instructions on how to build a toy aeroplane.

'Oh, Mummy, I love it,' he shouted, reached out to her

and gave her a hug.

'I don't remember ever having a birthday party,' mused Simon, looking pensively at his mother.

Margaret ran her fingers along her pearl necklace, thinking for a moment.

'We always had a cake on your birthday, but it was difficult with us moving around.'

Simon frowned. 'I see.'

'I remember when you were seven we bought you a Red Indian dressing-up suit, you loved it. You spent so much time in the bathroom looking at yourself in the mirror while you pretended to threaten imaginary people with your bow and arrow that the next birthday I bought you a full-length stand-alone mirror for your room. It was, of course, a very good thing because you've learnt excellent dress sense and now always look so well groomed.'

Simon chuckled and gave his mother a smile.

Jason pulled the huge box towards himself.

'It's from Holly,' said Cathy.

Jason tore off the paper and examined the picture on the box of a bright blue and yellow scooter.

'Oooh,' he said, jumping up and down. 'Open it, Mummy, open it!' Cathy opened the box, pulled the metal scooter out and adjusted it into position. Jason scooted round the kitchen. 'I love it, Mummy.'

'Goodness, what an expensive present for a six year old,' said Margaret.

'Yes, completely over the top in my opinion,' said Simon under his breath, 'but that's Holly all over, isn't it.'

What a mean thing to say, Cathy thought. I can't believe he's just said that, Holly's not like that at all.

'When can I go out on it?' asked Jason excitedly.

'Later, open the other presents first,' said Cathy. 'There are two more.'

Jason dumped the scooter on the ground and jumped up to the table. He opened another present from a friend, then came to a large envelope.

'That's from me,' said Simon. 'Last, but not least. Maybe the best. I think you'll be very pleased with this.'

Jason tore it open. He pulled out a piece of shiny cardboard and looked at it, bewildered. 'What is it?'

Cathy watched, feeling a hint of trepidation.

'It's tickets to next Saturday's football match, Chelsea against Arsenal,' beamed Simon. 'Just the two of us. That will be nice, won't it?'

Cathy took several deep breaths and bit her lip.

'Mummy's not coming?' Jason said, looking at her.

Cathy glanced at Simon, trying to read his expression, but he looked away and became absorbed in examining the tickets.

'It seems not,' she said.

'I want to go out on my scooter now.' Jason rode around the kitchen again.

'Just a quick ride before it gets dark,' said Cathy, keeping her voice as calm and light as she could. As she noticed the knot in her stomach, she became vaguely aware of her emotions, a chaotic, simmering mix of anger, disappointment and impotence.

'Please, Uncle Simon, will you take me?'

Simon beamed at Jason. 'Of course, I'd love to, we'll go in a few minutes.'

Jason scooted out of the kitchen, singing '*The wheels on the bus...* '

'I wish you'd told me about the tickets,' said Cathy quietly, hoping Margaret wouldn't hear.

'Why?' asked Simon at normal volume.

'It will be nice for Simon and Jason to spend time together,' butted in Margaret. 'What a lovely present. Maybe you and I could have a shopping trip instead when they're at the game. There's a chic little boutique I know in Watford with some clothes I think would suit you very nicely indeed.'

'Mother's right. What a good idea.'

'Oh... I suppose so,' Cathy said. A dreadful sinking feeling overwhelmed her, a kind of hopeless melancholy. I must look happy for Jason's sake, she thought.

CHAPTER 24

An Lac Monastery, Delat, Vietnam

Annando walked mindfully, as he always did. He wasn't fantasising or daydreaming, ruminating or planning; he wasn't thinking of the past, or the future. He was aware only of each foot stepping in front of the other, of the sound of each footfall on the dirt path, and also of the smell of early morning dew, the cool air on his exposed arms and the light feel of the brown cotton robes against his skin.

From behind he heard the regular footsteps of someone approaching. Annando stopped and turned, facing the brother; they bowed to each other.

'For you,' the bhikku, the Buddhist monk, said in Vietnamese, holding out an envelope. 'It arrived in the post yesterday.'

The sun rose behind the coconut palms casting long shadows on the neatly cut grass. Annando took the envelope and examined it. It was creased and had noticeable grubby fingermarks, the white paper tinged brown. The address, now faded, was written in English, in blue ink. It read 'Venerable Annando', at 'An Lac Monastery' followed by the address. He didn't recognise the neat, precise handwriting. It was postmarked Hampstead, United Kingdom, and from the date he could tell it had taken a few weeks for it to get to him.

Sunnido bowed respectfully and went on his way. Annando took the back route, down an orchid-strewn path, to his kuti, his small hut, close to the sala, the meeting hall. He strode up the two steps to his porch, took off his sandals and, as always, placed them neatly against the bamboo

152

wall before going inside and closing the door. He received a small but steady stream of foreign letters. Most were from people asking for his advice and guidance or wanting to visit. Sometimes they contained donations of cash or bank drafts. People asked for chants or blessings for the sickly or on the anniversary of a death. Often they were letters of thanks for his Dhamma, his teaching. Once an abusive letter told him to go home: Westerners were enemies and had destroyed their country. Westerners could not be Buddhists, especially not Buddhist monks.

Settling himself in his simple rattan chair, he opened the letter. When he read the name 'Cathy' he felt surprise and feelings of joy and affection. Although he had thought about her from time to time, it was only as a part of his past. But the words 'in difficulty' made him feel strange and uncomfortable. When he had finished, he read it again and then a third time, paying close attention to each word, mindfully noting the feelings that arose in him, which were unexpectedly and disconcertingly strong. He noticed that he was breathing deeply, something he hadn't consciously controlled. He sat there for a few moments in silence and looked through the window at the tamarind trees in the distance, observing the wave of emotion which surged from somewhere deep inside. What is this about, he thought? Why this reaction? Suddenly a whole raft of memories and images filled his consciousness. His heart beat strongly in his chest; this hadn't happened for a long time, for years. He sat back in his chair, closed his eyes and sighed. His equilibrium had been smashed.

He had shut himself off from the past, much of which he bitterly regretted and wanted to forget. He had provided for Cathy so she could get on with her life without him and he could pursue the path he had chosen with no regrets or distractions. He took a deep breath and rubbed his chin; there had always been a nagging feeling in the back of his mind that perhaps it wasn't as simple as that and couldn't be. Somewhere in the forest a monkey screeched. He got up and stood by the unglazed window looking towards the origin of the sound, watching for swaying branches or the sight of a primate swinging between the trees. This was something he'd done often over the years as a mindfulness practice to keep his awareness in the present moment, but today it didn't work, his mind was distracted. What mattered were his responsibilities here and now, in the monastery. There was no going back; how could he doubt it?

A lot had happened in the last six years. Annando's position of seniority in the Sangha, the community of Buddhist monks, had increased dramatically since his ordination and the Sangha relied on and looked up to him. It was only a year since Abbot Ajahn Kai Luat had died and he was surprised to have been selected as his successor. He was preparing to take on responsibilities as the new Abbot, slowly easing into the role. His responsibility to the monastery, and to the Sangha, was clear. And yet... something in the letter tugged at him, unravelling his clarity of thought and vision; he took another deep breath. As the hours went by he paced the kuti, although the few square yards did not offer much space; this was something that he had done, and then only rarely, over the years. However much he tried to bring his mind into focus, back to the present moment, Cathy was there, vital and alive in his thoughts. He remembered her voice, the way she laughed, the fall of her hair across her face, and in spite of his attempts to resist, he remembered the touch of her lips on his, the feel of her in his arms, the smoothness and warmth of her bare skin.

During the evening meditation Annando sat perfectly still as usual, but his mind wouldn't settle, the deep pool of silence hard to find. Lying on his bed afterwards, he found

154

himself unable to fall asleep. He was acutely aware of the object which lay under his bed, which he had not thought about in any depth for years. He had regularly pulled it out and cleaned behind and around it but it had remained for him a relic of a forgotten and buried past, almost as if it had nothing to do with him, that person who had a different name, dressed differently, spoke a different language, lived by different mores. Suddenly its significance had changed; it had become charged with energy, alive and vital. He could almost feel it pulsate under him, its hibernation over. The moonlight through the window bathed his kuti in a soft glow. A luminescent firefly danced against the bamboo walls; he watched it for a while, trying to be mindful. He got up and lit the candle on the centre of a metal saucer on his small table, then knelt on the floor beside his bed. Reaching his hand into the darkness under the wooden frame of the bed he drew out the small leather suitcase. When he had arrived at An Lac it was all he had brought with him. He put it on the mattress and felt for the clasps. With both thumbs pushing outwards they opened with a soft click. He lifted the lid. There was a smell of leather. Annando sat back in the chair and looked at the open case in silence for a long time as he struggled with conflicting desires, the desire to put the case back unopened and the desire to look at the contents. At last Annando sighed and gently leafed through the papers inside. He felt his passport and brought it out into the light. Flicking through the pages he found his photograph; a younger, dark-haired, intense-looking man stared back at him. He flicked through more pages, stamped with the authorisation of the many places he had travelled. There was a small black address book, legal papers and dictionaries: Cantonese, Thai, Vietnamese and French. It was a strange feeling, of things remembered but which belonged to another era, another space, a different man with a different name, a man called Blake,

155

Blake Carter, a man he recognised and remembered only hazily, as if in a cloud.

Eventually he found what he was looking for. He drew out the photograph of a brown-haired young woman. Her face was radiant with happiness as she grinned at the camera. He felt a sudden surge of nostalgia and melancholy. He looked at it for a long time and swallowed; there was a lump in his throat. 'Cathy,' he whispered into the night.

CHAPTER 25

Conway Place, Brandon Wood, North London

'Mummy, Mummy!' Jason, just home from an afternoon out with Simon, rushed over to the sofa where Cathy was watching the six o'clock news and jumped onto her lap.

'Golly, you are excited. Was it a good match?'

'Mummy, I scored a goal and so did Harry and Ivo and our team won,' he said in a rush.

'What, your team beat Harrow Primary School?'

'Yes!'

'Wonderful.'

He straddled her, looking her in the eye, vigorously bobbing up and down, his eyes sparkling.

'Well done you!'

'Surprise!' Simon came in and presented her with a huge bunch of tulips, red, orange and yellow. 'For my beautiful wife.'

She sniffed them. 'Oh, they're lovely.'

Simon came and sat close beside her, his arm around her shoulder.

'Uncle Simon saw me score the goal.'

Simon laughed. 'Yes, it was a good goal as well. Right in the corner.'

'I need to put these lovely flowers somewhere,' said Cathy.

'Give them to me.' He put the flowers at the other end of the sofa. 'You can put them in water later.'

'A corner goal,' said Cathy. 'Wow.'

Jason crawled across and gave Simon an uninhibited bear-hug, then jumped back on Cathy's lap.

'Mummy, I want a garden.'

'What?' Cathy frowned.

'Uncle Simon showed me this house with a garden.'

'When? When was this?' Cathy stiffened.

'Today,' said Simon cheerfully.

'Uncle Simon wants us to live there. I want to, too. Can we, Mummy?'

Cathy looked away but Jason grabbed her face in both his hands and made her look him straight in the eye.

'Please, Mummy.'

Cathy took a deep breath, her heart beating heavily. 'That's a lot for Mummy to think about.'

'Please, please, please!' His expression and tone of voice were insistent. 'Uncle Simon and I can play football in the garden all the time.'

Jason twisted off Cathy's lap, jumped down and on to the carpet and pretended to kick a ball. Simon sat back relaxed, his hands behind his head, and laughed.

'Please, Mummy.'

'I'm not thinking about that now, Jason. I'm watching the news.'

After a while Jason skipped off to his room, singing 'row, row, row your boat gently down the stream... '.

'It's just great seeing him happy, isn't it, darling.' Simon pulled her closer. Cathy tried to slide away.

'Why did you do that?' she asked.

'Do what?'

'Show him the house?'

Simon put his hands above his head and yawned.

'Well, we were passing and I thought it might help make up your mind. Do you remember Mark? He phoned, said the offer he had fell through so the Broomfield Way house is on the market again. I still think it's a brilliant opportunity for us.'

'It must have been on the market for six months or more. It's June now, and we saw it in January. Maybe there's something wrong with it.'

'No, Mark says the house is fine, it's just the buyers. They can't get mortgages.'

She shrugged.

'So I took Jason to have a look at it,' he said cheerfully.

'What's Jason got to do with this?'

'You thought Jason wasn't ready to move but he thinks he is.'

'He's a child. He can't make an informed decision, there are too many things to consider.'

'It looks like he's made an informed decision to me.'

Cathy felt a shudder of indignation pulse through her; she glared at him. 'That wasn't fair of you and it puts me under pressure. Last time you spoke to me about this you got angry, I just don't... ' She felt tears welling in her eyes.

He grabbed her hand, kissed it and put his arm around her in an affectionate embrace.

'I'm sorry, darling, maybe I was a bit hasty showing Jason, but... that other thing, I'll never do that unspeakable thing to you again, I promise. Look, there's no pressure on you, really. It's your decision entirely. I want you to be happy more than anything.' They sat in silence for a while. 'But you know, if we were to move, I wouldn't need to keep putting so much money away each month for the business. The workshop and office would be on the premises. I'd be in a better position to help with the bills.'

Cathy drew in her breath.

'Then you could use your salary to open that savings account for Jason. It's a win-win really.'

Cathy sighed and looked into the distance at a spot on the wall. She felt him kiss her tenderly on the cheek. In the background the TV news kept rolling. 'But only when you're ready, darling. I know you're scared of change, but I'll be happy to take control of everything.'

She frowned. 'I can cope, you know.'

'But, to be honest, you're not as resilient as you think you are, are you? You find change difficult, even good change. You're quite vulnerable really, but you don't like to confess it.'

Cathy had to admit to herself that there was some horrible element of truth in what he was saying.

'When the time comes I'll deal with everything. By the way, you look gorgeous in that floral dress Mother helped you choose and... ' He peered closely at her. 'Is that lipstick you're wearing? It's subtle, just a touch of pink but it suits you. You're such a beautiful lady, you really are. I'm so proud to call you my wife.'

Simon got up, hummed a tune and left the room. Cathy went and stood at the window. For a long time she watched as the wind pushed the clouds into feathery streaks and they rushed across the sky. Her mind was an empty vessel, strangely quiet, but, for some unfathomable reason, at the same time she felt as if she were being slowly strangled. Looking down, she vacantly watched the children playing in the park. Directly below, pedestrians were milling about, going on their way. In the street she noticed a man leaning on a lamppost, reading a newspaper. He wore a navy shirt and jeans; his face was obscured by a cap.

CHAPTER 26

'Hello, at last I've been able to come without Simon here.' Holly looked carefully at Cathy. 'I didn't want to leave you so long, especially in the circumstances.'

'I'm fine, Holly, really.'

Cathy stood upright with her shoulders back and smiled brightly as Holly came into the flat.

Holly took off her coat and hung it up in the hallway before slipping off her shoes.

'You look better.'

'Yes, the bruises are completely gone of course. It's been at least three months now since he did... you know what he did.' They went through to the kitchen. Cathy boiled the kettle and warmed a teapot. 'Tea?'

'Yes, darling, please.'

'I've got a Victoria sponge here. You like that, don't you?' said Cathy

'Did you buy a cake just for me?'

'Not just for you, I like it as well.'

'That would be delicious.'

Cathy prepared the teas.

'Go into the sitting room if you like, I'll bring it through.'

Holly went through to the sitting room and settled herself on the sofa. She's just a bit too upbeat, she thought. Am I seeing the real Cathy? Cathy brought in the tray of tea and cake.

'You're still wearing dresses, I see,' Holly said.

'Look, it's June, a dress is cool when the weather's hot and it has been, so that's fine.' She gave Holly her tea and cake and sat down herself. 'I wanted to tell you about Jason. He's doing so well now, he's even joining in rounders after school and he's mixing really well with the other children. I'm so pleased about it.'

'That's good, but what about you? You're the one I'm most concerned about.'

'I'm fine. Simon's been nice, on the whole. In fact, when he's nice, he's really nice. Brings me flowers and compliments me.' Cathy's voice was unusually light and sing-song. Her eyes were soft when she looked at Holly, but, Holly thought, somewhat evasive. 'Don't worry about me. I'm sure he'll never do that unspeakable thing to me again, I really am.' Cathy sat back and took a sip of her tea. 'Anyway, he's been away quite a bit. I think he's forgotten all about the mirror, bloody thing.' She put her hand to her mouth and giggled. 'He never mentions it. So, as you can see, everything is fine, really.' Cathy settled down into the armchair. 'By the way, Jason loves his scooter. Simon takes him to the park at the weekends to ride it. It was a really good choice. Well done. How about you?'

Holly sat back for a moment and looked at her friend.

'Cathy, are you sure? Please, be honest with me. How are you really feeling? Don't put on a front. It's me you're talking to. We know each other too well.'

Cathy looked up to the ceiling and sighed. 'It's OK. It's better, really. I'm trying to make it work. I have to believe it can work. My mother said relationships are all about compromise, and I need to try.'

'Your mother doesn't know Simon.'

'I can't give up, not yet.'

'Hmm…' They sat in silence for some moments. 'So, is Simon still wanting to move house?'

They quietly ate their cake.

'This is really good,' Cathy said. Looking down at her plate she mopped up a few crumbs with her finger and popped them in her mouth. 'Shame I didn't make it. I bought it from the baker down the road. I'll have to visit

162

there again.'

'Yes, it's delicious.' A few moments later Holly tentatively asked, 'What about the house, darling?'

Cathy sighed deeply. 'Oh, Holly…' and looked intently at her friend. 'I can't pretend with you so I won't try. I'm in such a dilemma.' She sighed again. 'This is Blake's flat, he gifted it to me. So I don't feel that it's mine to sell.'

'*Blake's* flat?'

'It was.'

'Go on.' Holly put down her cup of tea.

'Yes, he gave up everything when he went to Vietnam. Monks aren't supposed to have any possessions. He'd told me this but at the time I didn't even think about what he'd do with his money, his stuff. It didn't even cross my mind, I was just thinking about his going away, that was all I focused on. The emptiness, the devastation I was feeling. I didn't know about this flat until after he'd left. His solicitor told me. He just… ' She opened her arms wide, '… gave it to me. It was such a shock; I was bowled over, gobsmacked. Of course it's been a financial lifeline. God knows how I would have managed with Jason without it. When I thought about it later I wondered why he hadn't given it to one of his brothers… he has two. Why me? I kept asking myself over and over again. OK, it was a love affair but I never expected that… I love this flat… I feel close to him when I'm here. You must think I'm a bit mad I suppose.'

'You feel sentimental about it. It's full of memories.'

Cathy got up and paced around.

'It is. You know when he was living here, like a monk, he had hardly any possessions. All these years I've kept the flat like it was when he was living here, sort of empty, because it reminds me of him. That's why I found it so difficult when Simon moved his stuff in. The flat felt contaminated somehow, as if something precious had been

163

violated. It's completely irrational, I know, because I invited Simon in. God, I sound bonkers... but that's the way it is.'

'No, I can understand that. I wondered why the only room you bothered with was Jason's.'

'I feel his presence here. I'm just not ready to move.' She looked pained.

'I can understand that, in the circumstances.'

'I *could* sell it of course, it's mine legally.'

'If you don't want to move, don't. Simple. I'm concerned about what Simon did, concerned about your welfare.'

'I think it's going to be OK.'

Holly sighed. 'Look, I don't want to be the bearer of bad news, but they say once a wife-beater, always a wife-beater.'

'That can't be right; I just don't believe that,' Cathy said vehemently.

'He hurt you, hit you, Cathy. Left you bruised. Surely you can't accept that?'

'He slapped me, Holly, that's all. Just one random moment of anger. Don't make more of it than it is.'

Holly shook her head. 'You've forgiven him?'

'Yes, I had to, he's my husband.' She looked frightened suddenly. 'But I haven't forgotten.'

'Nor have I.'

'You see, I've been thinking, Simon's right, it would be good for Jason to have a garden. I'm the one being inflexible. I need to do the best thing for Jason.'

'No, you need to do the best thing for you. If you're unhappy Jason will be unhappy in the long term, I promise you,' said Holly forcefully.

Cathy sat perched on the edge of her seat and ran her fingers through her short hair.

'Well, I just know at the moment I can't make any big

decisions like that; I'm used to everything, the neighbours, all I need is convenient and local. He's not pressurising me, really.'

'Good, you tell him firmly, you're not ready to move, stand up for yourself.'

'I will, really I will.'

'I bloody hope so… Talking of neighbours, that reminds me, who's living next door?'

'That's Doreen, an elderly lady, she's lost the plot a bit, forgetful, a bit dotty, but she's in hospital at the moment.'

'How long has she been in hospital?

'A few weeks.'

'Does she have any family?'

'She has a son, Alan. Why?'

'I'll tell you in a minute... what is he like?'

Cathy looked up to the ceiling, thinking.

'Nice, nondescript.'

'Nothing… memorable about Alan?'

'No, he's small, a bit plump.'

'Right, and who lives on the top floor?'

'The flat directly above is empty; the one opposite has a Japanese couple in it. They're renting. He works for a bank in the city somewhere. Anyway, why?'

Holly looked thoughtful for a moment.

'Because just as I was coming up the stairs I noticed this man in a baseball cap, youngish, tall and fit, in jeans, on his way down. I didn't see his face but I'm sure I hadn't seen him before. I just wondered which flat he was coming out of.'

'No idea, no one I know.' Cathy shrugged her shoulders. 'Look, it's a lovely day now, the sun has come out, shall we go for a walk.'

'Good idea.'

CHAPTER 27

'This flat is falling apart. I can't get the key in the bloody lock.' Simon slammed the front door shut behind him. 'I've been outside for five minutes fiddling about with it. Didn't you hear me ringing the bell?' His tone was thick with irritation, his face flushed.

Cathy stiffened; she'd heard that tone of voice before. 'No, I've been in the bathroom.'

He looked up and down the corridor. 'Jason's not here tonight, is he?'

'No… he's with Billy.'

He grunted. 'First the boiler, now the lock.' Simon hurriedly unlaced his shoes and placed them neatly on the mat. 'You haven't had a problem then?'

She thought for a moment.

'I did have a problem with it yesterday, now you mention it. It seemed a bit stiff.'

'I don't want to invite any other workmen round to fix it, do I?' As he looked at her his eyes narrowed, 'Knowing your track record.'

Cathy flinched. 'I can't believe you just said that. That was a really horrible thing to say.'

Simon looked sheepish suddenly. 'Yes, I suppose it was a bit below the belt. But look, this whole bloody flat is falling apart and I've had a fucking awful day driving around in the heat.' He huffed. 'There's been another offer on the house at Broomfield Way. Have you thought about moving yet?'

She glared at him. 'I'm not ready. Don't ask me again.'

'Oh, for God's sake, you're such a procrastinator. I don't want to be stuck in this bloody flat for the next ten years.'

Cathy bristled.

'We've only been married nine months and all you've done is pressurise me to move since day one! I thought you were going to buy your own home but you can't, can you? Sometimes I just feel like a cash cow.'

Simon thumped his fist against the wall, gritted his teeth and gave her a look that sent shivers down her spine. Cathy retreated into the bedroom but Simon was close behind. He slipped off his sports jacket and flung his briefcase on the floor. Her heart beat rapidly; she slunk into a corner and turned away, her face in her hands. She could hear him breathing heavily and heard him undo his belt. She froze. Suddenly she felt his hands tightly on her shoulders; he twisted her towards him and backed her roughly against the wall.

'Come on, Cathy, I want us try out this mirror. I've been patient so far, haven't I?'

'Simon, I've told you, I don't want to. You forced it on me.' Her voice trembled, she was stiff with fear. 'Anyway, you're angry; this is no time to be making love.'

'You won't move house, you won't try the mirror, what else won't you bloody do?'

There was a hint of liquor in his hot breath on her cheek and he smelt of sweat. He had one hand hard on her shoulder; his other hand he plunged between her legs, roughly massaging her crotch. She rammed against him, using all her physical strength to push him away.

'Jason is coming home. Stop!'

'Not tonight. He's staying the night with Billy. Remember? Think I'm stupid?' He stared at her with angry eyes. 'Jason didn't see you with the plumber, did he?' he growled. 'You arranged that OK. I want the light on, I want to see you naked and submissive and panting.'

With a quick thrust Cathy kneed him hard in the groin.

'Ouch,' he cried, releasing his grip of her, bent over and

167

brought his hands between his legs. Stumbling, he took a step backwards. 'Bitch,' he spat and some saliva dripped down his chin.

For a brief moment they stood there staring at each other. Simon's eyes were feverish, flashing fire. She shuddered. Suddenly he lifted his arm and struck her across the face. Cathy felt the sharp pain of the slap and brought her hand to her cheek.

Simon was breathing heavily, looking at her wildly.

'It's your fault; you mustn't push me, Cathy.'

'You said you wouldn't,' she moaned, in disbelief that he'd hit her. She put her hand to her hot, stinging cheek.

Simon stood there for a few moments, panting, rooted to the spot, then, like a chameleon, slowly his expression changed, his features becoming soft and affectionate. He took a step towards her.

'I'm sorry, darling, I was angry, I said some bad things, I never meant to do that... you're hurt. I was wrong. I'll make it up to you,' he said endearingly, his expression full of wretchedness and regret.

'Get out, just go... go,' she shouted.

He slowly walked away and she heard the front door close.

Cathy stumbled to the bathroom and splashed cold water on her face. Oh God, Jason mustn't ever see this, she thought, and stifled a sob. I can't believe he did that, she said to herself over and over again, her hands shaking.

* * *

Out on the pavement the road was busy with the lights of the evening traffic, the splash of car wheels on puddles and the rush of evening commuters. Simon took a few deep breaths and fastened his belt. He walked on past shops and side-roads. It happened so quickly Simon didn't see who pulled him into the dark alleyway where there was a smell of garbage and rotting food. The man had grabbed him from behind and pinned his wrists behind his back; he felt an arm around his neck holding him tightly as if in a vice. He could hardly breathe. He heard a click and something sharp was pushed against his neck. Simon shivered suddenly; he felt his heart thud in his chest. The voice in his ear was smooth and steady.

'You leave her alone. Threaten her again and you'll have to answer to me. Do you understand, Simon Scott?' Simon felt the cold metal being pressed hard on his neck. He gasped for breath.

'Yes,' he whispered.

'Louder!'

'Yes!' Simon shouted.

Simon was released and the man melted away into the darkness. Simon stumbled, coughed and steadied himself against the wall, his legs like jelly. Panting, he looked around the dingy alleyway. Bags of garbage were piled high; bottles and cans lay discarded in corners. When he had caught his breath he stumbled back into the bright lights and the busy street, his heart pounding.

CHAPTER 28

Cathy opened the door. Jason was standing on the doormat with Holly behind him, her hands resting gently on his shoulders.

'Why didn't you get me, Mummy?' Jason looked up at his mother, then tilted his head and stared, wide-eyed. 'Mummy, your face is black, why?'

'Nothing, darling,' she mumbled, patting her cheek and trying to ignore the lump in her throat. 'Mummy just had a little accident. Thanks for picking him up, Holly.' She looked over at Holly, who silently mouthed 'bastard' and shook her head.

'Holly, please come in.' Cathy squatted down and unfastened Jason's coat. 'You go and play with your counting blocks while I chat to Auntie Holly.'

'But Mummy, why is your face black? Will it always be black?'

'It's not really black, just a little red.'

'But why?'

He reached with his finger and touched it.

Cathy flinched. 'No, best not to touch it too much.'

'Does it hurt?'

'Only a little. I'll look just as I did soon, I promise.'

'Where's Uncle Simon?'

Cathy cringed at the sound of his name. She took a deep breath and bit her lip.

'He's not here.'

'Oh, but I want him to play with me.'

'Not today, darling... I'll make you a banana milkshake. That'll be nice, won't it? Run along now and play. I'll tell you when it's ready.'

'OK, Mummy.' Jason walked quietly to his bedroom,

his shoulders slumped.

Cathy beckoned Holly into the kitchen. 'Thank you,' she said quietly. 'I couldn't bear it if the other mothers saw me like this. As it's summer, I can get away with wearing sunglasses and a sunhat, but even so... there's a dreadful gossip at the school gate.'

'It was lucky I was working nearby. I'm glad I wasn't in Nottingham or anywhere else. When did this happen?'

'Yesterday. I'd already arranged for Jason to spend the night with Billy, so Billy's mother collected him from school.'

'Jason wasn't here when...'

'No.'

'But what if Jason had been here?' asked Holly.

'No, no, I won't even think about that. Don't go there...' said Cathy, gesticulating wildly.

'OK, leave it...' Holly took a deep breath and peered at Cathy, her expression full of concern. 'Anyway, have you seen a doctor?'

Cathy shook her head. 'No, no, I couldn't. The shame.'

'Well, I think you're making a mistake; you should go.'

'I can't, Holly.'

'It does look bad. Here, let me see.' Holly examined her. 'What have you put on it?'

'Just some moisturising cream. It isn't so painful anymore so I suppose it's healing.' Suddenly Cathy put her hands over her face and stifled a sob. 'It's not the injury that's the worst, but it's so terrible, this pretending. I have to, for Jason. What do I tell him?' Cathy looked at Holly, her expression distraught. 'I've told him so many lies, Holly, it kills me, kills me inside.' She patted her chest. 'I ask myself, what sort of mother am I?'

Holly took a step back and put her hands on her hips. 'Look, where is Simon now?'

'I don't know... the pub I expect, or sulking with his

171

mother… Look, after he'd done... you know what…' she grimaced and sniffed. 'He'd been drinking... he was sorry straight away, as he always is, then he went out, and when he came back, this is the weird thing, he was really different, he seemed scared of something, there was real fear in his voice. I don't know what came over him. Said he'd never do it again and that he'd be on the road for a few days, Manchester and Harrogate, with work. Then he was gone. I expect he spent last night with his mother.'

'Bastard. You don't believe it, all that grovelling, do you?'

'I'd like to but... not really, no.' She frowned.

'You could get the locks changed.'

'Maybe.'

'Have you thought of moving out?'

'Then what do I tell Jason? I take him to some godforsaken hostel and say this is our new home and you'll never see Uncle Simon again? He adores Uncle Simon.'

'You're not going to take him back are you, after this?'

Cathy was silent for a moment.

'I'm not sure what to do.' She spoke with averted eyes, trying not to look Holly in the face. 'He's my husband. I feel loyalty towards him, whatever he's done. I need to give him a chance, for Jason's sake.'

'You cannot be serious.'

'I married him, Holly, that matters. Matters to me. He took me on, with Jason, who is not his son, gave me security, respectability. It's important, Holly.'

Holly shook her head.

'Cathy, you're an independent woman earning your own money, you don't need him to validate you. Please, we're not living in the seventeenth century…'

'I know,' said Cathy.

'I hope so. Know it and believe it. I know what I'd do but I'm not you, Cathy. It all needs time and careful

172

consideration… but with Simon behaving like this something has to be done.'

'I don't want people to see me like this.'

'So… what are you going to do about work?'

'I phoned in sick. A couple of days and it will look better I hope. I've still got some concealer I used last time, no one will notice.'

'This can't go on.'

Cathy took a deep breath.

'No, it can't and it won't. I'm going to show him he needs to compromise and that I can assert myself. Anyway, look, I've armed myself, in case of emergency.' She beckoned Holly into the hallway and showed her, hidden behind some coats on the coat stand, a wooden rolling pin leaning against the wall. 'I'll knock him out.'

Holly shook her head incredulously. 'I'm not sure that's a solution; he might grab it from you, anything could happen… '

'Oh, don't say that. I don't expect I'll ever have the opportunity or the guts to use it; and I won't need to. It's just precautionary, it makes me feel better. I can look after myself and Jason, really I can. I will not be forced out of my home. It's my son, my home,' she said decisively. 'I'm determined now and empowered. It's taken me a long time to see this clearly. You've done that for me, Holly, and I'm grateful.'

'I like you talking like this. I'm relieved you've found some inner strength, but in my opinion giving him another chance is madness.' She twisted her emerald ring between her fingers.

'I have to,' Cathy said quietly. 'I have to believe that we can make it work. Maybe I need to make some changes, to accommodate him. I have to try.'

Holly shook her head, crossed her arms and looked doubtfully at her friend. 'Cathy, please see the reality…

he's not going to change.'

Cathy opened her arms wide. 'But I can. Look, have you noticed? I'm back in my jeans and T-shirt. That's a statement of independence in itself.'

'I did notice... and I'm very pleased about it.'

'Simon and I, we will work it out. Marriage needs working at.' In his bedroom Jason was singing. They heard the sound of wooden blocks being piled up. 'Good, I'm pleased he's singing again, it means he's happy. Look, I need to make Jason his milkshake,' said Cathy, getting the blender and bananas ready.

'I respect your choice, reluctantly, but I'm worried about you.' Holly held both hands on the back of a chair, her lips pursed. 'You call me the moment he makes contact, understand.'

'Yes, I promise I will. He's too interested in his reputation to do something more stupid to me.'

'Don't bank on it, but let's hope you're right. From what I know he wants to keep up the façade, the image he's cultivated of the successful, sophisticated man about town.' She took a deep breath. 'What crap. But this might change if he's angry or drunk or both. Take care.'

'Don't worry about me, Holly. I'm fine, really.'

* * *

Cathy selected her dowdiest, floppiest trousers and a grey high-necked shirt, buttoned at the neck, took a swig of whisky and waited for the bell to ring. Standing tall and gathering her courage she opened the door with a flourish. Two burly men in boiler suits stood there.

'Mrs Scott,' said the smaller, older man in a gruff voice.

'Yes, come in.' Cathy took a step back and the men came in, wiping their boots on the mat.

'It's a mirror you want removing.'

'That's right. I only moved in three weeks ago and it certainly isn't something I'd want. Not in that position anyway.'

She stood there awkwardly for a moment. The men looked at her, waiting.

'This way.'

She led them into the bedroom and bit her lip. They looked around.

'Where is it?' the older man asked.

Cathy cleared her throat. Looking away, she pointed to the ceiling.

'Oh,' sniggered the younger man. 'Well then.'

The older man wolf whistled.

'Some people are peculiar,' said Cathy, feeling her face flushed with heat. 'I didn't meet the couple who lived here before but they had some very strange stuff in here, really bohemian.'

'It's a biggun,' said the older man, grinning. 'Take some getting down, might leave a few holes in the ceiling.'

'Please, just take it away,' said Cathy.

'Mick, bring the steps from the van, will you.'

The younger man went out. Out of the corner of her eye she saw the older man looking at her sceptically, scanning her up and down, his lip curling slightly. Cathy wished the earth would swallow her up.

'I'll let you get on with it then,' she said and hurried out of the room.

CHAPTER 29

Standing at the sink, Cathy dried some cups with a tea towel.

'You know, darling, I've been meaning to talk to you about something.' Simon stretched with his hands behind his head and his legs straightened in the wicker chair. 'It's... er... not the mirror. You were right to take it down if it made you uncomfortable. I was too pushy, inconsiderate. I realise that now.'

She stopped for a moment and looked at him.

'I'm so glad you said that. It means a lot. I'm so much happier now it's gone.'

Simon sat silently for a few moments.

'I didn't want to remind you, us, of that time when I... behaved badly. I know it's a few weeks ago now and I'm mortified and disgusted with myself. I'm so sorry, darling. I know we haven't talked about it since, but I wanted to say, sincerely, I'll never do it again... and I am trying. I hope you've noticed how I've changed, trying to put you first.'

He's been like a different man the last few weeks, thought Cathy. And now he's opened up about it. Maybe we've turned a corner; God, I hope so.

'I know,' said Cathy. 'You've been so nice since.'

'But there's something that's been bothering me.'

His expression stiffened and he crossed his arms.

'What's that? 'she said with a sense of trepidation.

'Well... after I left the building that evening... after I behaved badly, I was just walking along the road and I was threatened, believe it or not, pulled into an alleyway. Did you know that?' Simon changed his posture and sat forward, perched on the end of the chair.

'Threatened, who threatened you, how?' She shrugged. 'How could I know, you didn't mention it at the time?'

'Some man.' Simon's face flushed and his expression changed to one of fear. 'I was a bit shocked, needed time to think about what happened. He grabbed me from behind.'

'Why on earth?'

'Told me to keep away from you.' He looked directly at her.

'What!' She stopped drying in mid-motion, tea towel in one hand, cup in the other, and stared at him, wide-eyed.

'Who is he?' asked Simon, his eyes narrowing.

'I've got no idea. Are you kidding me?' Cathy's heart raced.

'I think what happened is this,' he said, staring at her, stock still. 'After our small argument and I'd left, you phoned someone... and they accosted me.'

She dropped the cup on the floor, where it bounced and rolled onto its side.

'Phoned someone – don't be ridiculous!'

'I didn't see his face, but I heard his voice, a smooth talker, cold, menacing.'

'I don't know what you're talking about.'

'Of course what I did was terrible, I know that, but... don't play games with me; you hired someone, didn't you, a professional to scare me off.' His voice was slow and controlled.

'Simon, I don't know who it was, I swear.'

Cathy felt as if she was burning up suddenly.

'I don't like being threatened and I don't like being lied to.' His eyes glazed over and his face turned a deep shade of red; he rubbed his chin. 'You're quite a dark horse, aren't you?'

'This is mad. I don't know what you're talking about!'

'There are things about you I don't know. Like how you came to buy this flat, when even your mother doesn't know where you got the money... yes, she told me so on the phone.' His teeth were gritted tight.

'Simon, you're frightening me, please.'

'So, who threatened me?'

'I really don't know, swear to God.'

Suddenly his face softened and his body relaxed. 'I believe you. I'm sorry, darling. It's been playing on my mind, it wasn't nice.' He relaxed back in his chair and looked up at the ceiling for a few moments. 'So... there must be another explanation. Is there anyone else you've spoken to about our argument?'

Cathy took a deep breath; she felt she might faint.

'I might have done, I'm entitled to. You were drunk, in a furious mood, and you hurt me. Besides, it's none of your business whom I talk to.'

'It becomes my business if I'm threatened.'

He stared at her, his eyes cold.

'I don't know who threatened you. How could I?'

He studied her carefully and his face relaxed.

'No, I don't believe you do. I've made lots of mistakes.' He shook his head. 'I'd had a bad day, said terrible things to you, I was a bit drunk and... I should never have hit you, never. Forgive and forget? Please?' His expression was repentant.

Cathy gulped. 'It's difficult. I need time.' She put her hand to her heart. 'The last time you looked at me as you did a few moments ago you hit me.'

Simon got up and came close to her; he tried to embrace her but she slid away.

'I will never hit you again, I swear. I love you so much, you and Jason, more than I can say.'

'Then maybe I could be alone with Jason for the night. Do you mind, it's been stressful for both of us lately. Give us some space.'

He frowned. 'Where do you expect me to go?'

'To your mother's.'

He drew his breath in.

'Well, that's not easy, she'll wonder why.'

'Please.'

He stood for a while staring into the distance; a moment later he caught her eye.

'I'll do this for you, darling, of course,' he said affectionately. 'I'll have to think of a good excuse.'

CHAPTER 30

'Why is that man there, Mummy?' Jason pointed out of the open sash window into the street below.

'What man?'

'The man with the hat.' He gestured for her to come over. 'The one reading a book.'

Cathy came to the window.

'Look, that man.' He pointed again.

In the park children were playing and there was the noise of traffic up and down the road. On the street below a man in a cap and a navy shirt was leaning, relaxed, against the lamppost, head down, reading a paperback.

'I don't know, darling, maybe he's waiting for someone.'

Jason looked up at her, his bright eyes full of enthusiasm.

'Will you play trains with me again, like the other day?'

'What, now, darling?'

'Yes, Mummy, now.'

'Yes, of course.'

He took her hand and led her down the corridor. In his bedroom, the train set, on a low wide table, took up a good portion of the space. She looked around. It is a lovely room, she thought. She remembered painstakingly decorating it, to make it cosy and bright. The walls were light blue and covered with stick-on cartoon characters: Mickey Mouse, The Flintstones, Tom and Jerry. The lilac curtains were covered with pictures of teddy bears, the orange carpet was thick and soft. Jason pressed the switch to the motor and two neat little engines burst into life and rolled along the track.

'Let's have a race,' he said. 'You be the red one, I'll be

green.'

He attached the engines to the carriages. He pressed a switch and his engine with four green carriages whistled and whirled into action. His face lit up with pleasure. They played, absorbed in the game for a while until the trains rolled into the stations and the bells rang. Jason took a carriage in his hand and examined it, rolling the wheels in his hand. Then he picked up a little figure of a man and placed him on the platform at the station.

'Look, Mummy, he's waiting for someone as well,' he said, looking up at her.

It was an odd thing for Jason to say; it made her twitch, and she stopped for a moment. There was something stirring in her, there were questions, things that didn't make sense. Unless, unless...

She was staring into the distance. Jason grabbed her arm and shook it.

'Mummy, come on, you're not playing... '

Distracted, Cathy raced trains with him for some time until she let Jason win; he became bored and grabbed his abacus and blocks.

'Play with this now, Mummy,' he said, waving his abacus in front of her.

'Just a minute, darling, I need to do something.'

Cathy got up, raced to the living room window and looked out. The evening sun was setting on the horizon and the sky was turning a hazy shade of pink. The man was gone. She stood for a few moments reflecting, remembering and thinking. No, surely... Trembling, she felt from somewhere a surge of energy. OK, where to begin? She lifted up the cushions on the sofa one by one and examined them carefully, picked up the side lamp and looked underneath it then put it back. She lifted the rug, examined it, and slid it back in position. She stood still for a few moments, her heart palpitating wildly, her mind in a whirl, then, looking about, walked into the hallway. She looked carefully at the front door, opened it and examined the lock; it was stiff but functioning. She lifted the fitted hallway carpet, which was loose at the corner, yanked it clean away as far as she could and looked underneath. The underlay was still intact, fixed to the floor. She turned each shoe upside down and shook it. She ran her hand underneath each shelf of the dresser and looked inside each drawer. She went into the nearby cloakroom and pulled out the vacuum cleaner, the broom, the dustpan and brush and the laundry basket, then taking a torch she thoroughly examined every corner of the space. Still trembling a little, she examined every coat in turn and checked each pocket.

'Mummy, why are you making such a noise, what are you doing?' Jason stood before her holding a wooden block in one fist and his abacus in the other hand. 'Why are you shaking?'

Cathy suddenly realised how ridiculous she must look and how irrational she was being. She pulled herself together.

'Nothing, darling. I'll stop now, it isn't important,' she said.

He grabbed her hand. 'We haven't finished playing the game yet,' he said as he led her back into his bedroom.

CHAPTER 31

Distracted, Cathy went to the door and opened it. Simon stood there, red-faced and scowling, his tie askew, the top button of his shirt undone.

'I've forgotten my key.'

She smelt alcohol on his breath.

'Oh no.' Cathy tried to push it shut but Simon shot his foot out and stuck it in the doorway. 'You're not coming in drunk.'

'You've been trying to keep me away, haven't you? Just one night you said, then two, then three. I want to be in my own home.'

Cathy groaned with the strain as she tried to put her weight against the door but he was too strong and forced his way in. She backed against the wall, breathing heavily.

'Not very friendly, is it? Asking me to stay away for days and hiring a detective to follow me.' He smoothed his tie.

'What? I don't know what you're talking about!'

'But you're going to be on your best behaviour, aren't you, you're not going to lie, cheat, behave like a tart or give me any reason to be cross or impatient with you, are you? Because, however crap this flat is, this is my home.'

He took off his jacket, hung it up and walked briskly into the living room. Heart thumping, she followed him. Bending down, he yanked the telephone cable out of the wall, carried the phone to the kitchen and threw it violently in the bin. There was a loud crash.

'See... there... ' he said, pointing, his face red. 'No phoning for help, no detective rescuing you now, my love.'

Back in the living room Simon poured himself a neat whisky into a glass from a nearly empty decanter, gulped it

183

down in one and refilled it, gulped again and banged the empty glass heavily on the table.

Suddenly, in a furious rage, he lurched at her and stumbling, pinned her arms against the wall.

'Get me another drink, for God's sake,' he spat, and abruptly backed off, releasing her.

Trembling, Cathy went into the kitchen, with Simon following; she searched the liquor cupboard.

'I haven't got any more.'

'Look again, woman, look before I spank you.'

Cathy gulped and pretended to look for whisky. Suddenly angry, she felt emboldened. 'I don't like your language; don't talk to me like that. There isn't any, like I told you.'

'Bloody liar!' He spat and specks of saliva hit the table. He rubbed his mouth with the back of his hand. 'I don't like being conned,' he said. 'You want to know what it's like, having a man pin you down.'

He grabbed her and held her tight against the wall for what seemed like an age. He was breathing deeply and she felt the developing bulge in his crotch as he pushed himself against her.

'Let me go!' With all of her energy she pushed hard against him. He released her, stepped back and laughed menacingly.

'I'll find the whisky. It's here somewhere. Then I'll be ready, I've waited long enough, it's time.'

Shaking, Cathy rushed back into the living room; she could hear Simon swearing and clattering around in the kitchen as he searched for the liquor. 'Help me!' she whispered urgently into the empty space as if her life depended on it. 'Where are you, if you can hear me... ' she panted, 'I need you now! Please!'

A few minutes passed before Cathy heard a noise at the front door; it suddenly burst open, a man stormed in.

Rushing past Cathy, who in her desperate state had only a vague impression of him, he grabbed Simon, put him in an armlock, frog-marched him out of the flat and down the stairs. It had all happened so fast she barely had time to catch her breath before they were gone. Exhausted, Cathy collapsed on the floor and wailed.

CHAPTER 32

The man had his arm around Simon's neck. He pushed him out of the flat, down the stairs and out into the fading evening light. The stranger held him in a vice-like grip. With his arms pulled behind him, Simon trembled, gasping for breath. Outside, the stranger loosened his grip, said 'Walk' and prodded him along the pavement. Simon obeyed; the voice demanded it. They went around a corner and into a quiet street, stopping at a car parked at the kerb. He felt a pair of handcuffs being deftly clicked on his wrists. The man opened the front passenger door. 'Get in,' he said, pushing Simon into the seat. 'Don't move or say a word.' The voice was so smooth and controlled it made Simon shiver. He daren't turn around, daren't look at the man's face. Expertly, Simon was blindfolded, thrust into complete blackness, and something like glasses were perched on his nose. He felt tugging across his chest, he was being tied firmly to the seat. The passenger door slammed shut. Moments later the driver's door opened.

'You're making a big mistake,' Simon spluttered as the man settled himself in the seat. Simon felt a tremor run through him, his heart thumping, as the car sped off. The man didn't reply.

After what seemed like an hour, Simon felt the car lurch as it pulled off the road and bumped along an unmade track. The car came to a stop and the ignition was turned off. The man yanked Simon out of the car, nudged him in the back and marched him downhill for a long way over what felt underfoot like tree roots and stones. He heard owls hooting and felt a cool chill in the air and the smell of pine. Eventually they stopped.

'What's happening,' asked Simon, trembling.

'I'm leaving you here.'

'Where am I? How can I get back?' Simon heard the panic in his own voice.

He shuddered.

'I'm warning you for the last time.' The voice was quiet and controlled. 'If I ever find you anywhere near Cathy again, it will be the worse for you. This is just a taster. I can put you where no one will ever find you. Understand?'

Simon nodded, his mouth suddenly dry. 'Yes,' he said. He felt a tug and pull on his wrists and heard the handcuffs being unlocked, then his wrists were tied loosely with something rough that felt like rope. He heard soft footsteps heading away into the undergrowth. With shaking hands he fumbled with the rope and, after what seemed an interminable length of time, freed himself. As he removed the glasses and blindfold he peered into the darkness. There was enough dim light from the moon for him to see tall, dark, menacing trees, almost covering a slate-coloured grey sky. The cool evening air of the forest chilled him. He shivered, his heart beating hard in his chest. He began to walk, picking his direction at random.

CHAPTER 33

Cathy was on the floor. She curled into a foetal position with her face against her knees, breathing deeply and heavily. Time passed, maybe many hours, she didn't know. 'Thank you, benevolent life-force, for sparing Jason from seeing this, thank you, thank you,' she muttered over and over. A mixture of the terrible and the wonderful were rolled into one; it was too big to fathom for her small life, and it was all too quick. She knew only that something was over and something else had begun. She'd thought about him so much, remembered him, imagined him, given him qualities he didn't have, clouded her own memories in so many fantasies that he had become surreal. Her surreal, other-worldly monk... her spymaster... her one and only true love. She rolled on to her side and gradually uncurled. She straightened her arms and legs and stretched, picked herself up off the living room floor and slowly stood up. In the bathroom she splashed cold water on her face; looking in the mirror she despaired at the sight of her own reflection, her face flushed, her hair tangled and unkempt, her eyes puffy. God, I look awful, she thought. The doorbell rang and she flinched, her heart thumping. She stood there transfixed by her own image, trembling. There was an insistent knock at the door.

'Cathy.' She recognised Holly's voice shouting from outside and sighed, heavily and thankfully, with relief.

She splashed cold water on her face and dried it vigorously with a towel. At the front door she consciously stood up straight and forced a smile.

'Hello, Mummy.' Jason rushed in, clutching a big orange-coloured toffee-apple on a stick. 'Auntie Holly bought this for me.'

'Oh, how nice,' said Cathy. 'But you can't eat that now; it's late, time for bed.'

Jason skipped into his bedroom.

'What has happened? Are you OK?' whispered Holly, frowning.

'Yes, I'm fine, just a bit of a headache.'

'Come on, I'm not a fool. I'd better come in.'

There was the sound of footsteps on the stairs and Holly turned around.

'Someone's coming... no... no...' gasped Cathy, her hands on her cheeks.

'What is it?' asked Holly.

'I'm just twitchy, that's all. Who's coming?' Cathy strained to look down the stairwell. 'See who it is.'

Holly frowned. 'Are you expecting someone? Simon?'

First they saw the back of his bald head. Cathy gasped. She saw he had the same build as the stranger at the lamppost, wore the same navy shirt. Cathy's heart beat fast, pounding in her chest; she felt almost faint as if she could hardly breathe. As he turned the bend in the stairs they saw him face on. Oh, my God, it is, it is him, my Blake, my Blake, thought Cathy. Her head swam slightly, her knees buckled under her and she grabbed the edge of the door to keep upright. He reached the top step. As he came towards them, along the landing hallway, he slowed his pace and looked at Holly inquisitively and then intensely at Cathy. She put her hand to her heart and took several deep breaths. He stopped a few feet away from them. For a few moments they both looked at him in silence.

Eventually, with a rasp in her voice, Holly said, 'You must be Blake.'

'And you must be Holly,' said Blake. His voice was smooth and deep.

'You both....' Cathy looked from one to another.

'It's OK, I'll explain,' said Blake as he looked tenderly

at Cathy.

'Hmm... well I need to go and... I'm sure you have a lot of catching up to do,' said Holly as she made her way down the stairs.

'Yes,' said Cathy softly, moving aside as Blake came in; she gently closed the door behind them.

CHAPTER 34

'Who is this man, Mummy?' Jason looked up at the stranger standing in the hallway.

'This is your... er... ' Cathy cleared her throat. 'This is a friend of mine: Blake, Uncle Blake,' she said breathlessly, her heart palpitating wildly.

Jason looked at his mother, then at Blake, then at his mother again.

'I want Uncle Simon to play trains with me. Where is Uncle Simon?'

'Uncle Simon isn't here, he's had to go away, for work,' gulped Cathy.

Jason stared at Blake wide-eyed and after a short while he said, 'Do you want to see my train set, Uncle Blake?'

'Yes, I do.' Blake squatted down and looked Jason in the eye, smiling warmly. 'Show me your trains.'

'Will you play trains with me?'

'Yes, I'd like that,' said Blake.

Jason grabbed Blake's hand and led him into his bedroom, switched on the motor, which purred into life, and the trains ran round the track. Cathy leant against the doorway to Jason's room and watched as Blake, sitting cross-legged, played with him. She felt a lump in her throat and a flush to her cheeks. There was a similarity round the nose and mouth and their skin tone was the same. The conversation between them flowed fluidly and naturally as if they had always been together. They talked about Jason's school day and his toys and his interests. He showed Snowy to Blake, and let him hold it.

'Here, I got this book for my birthday. Will you read it to me? I can read, but I like it when someone else reads,' said Jason.

Jason thrust *The Tiger Who Came for Tea* into his hand and climbed onto Blake's lap.

'This looks like a nice book, yes, I would like to read it with you.'

As Jason turned the pages Blake read and Jason listened, absorbed.

Two or three books later, Jason said, 'When are you coming again, Uncle Blake?'

When Blake looked up he saw Cathy's eyes were full of tears. He said, 'Well, that depends on your Mummy.'

'I want you to come again,' said Jason. 'Please, Mummy.'

Cathy fought back tears.

Blake said, 'I will need to talk to your Mummy about that.'

Jason peered at Blake's shaven scalp.

'Uncle Blake, why haven't you got any hair?'

'I shaved it off.'

'Shaved it off?'

'Yes, that's right.'

'Can I feel it?'

'Yes, you can.' Blake bent forward and Jason ran his hand over Blake's shaven head.

'It feels funny,' Jason giggled, jumped off Blake's lap and went back to his trains.

'I'll talk to Uncle Blake now,' said Cathy gently. 'Get into your pyjamas and I'll come and tuck you in soon.'

Blake followed her into the living room.

CHAPTER 35

'Why are you here?' Cathy paced the living room, picking her nails, trying to avoid his gaze. 'I'm confused.'

'Yes, I expect you are.' Blake stood with his back against a wall. His expression was full of affection and contrition.

Cathy put her hands on her cheeks. 'You know her, Holly?'

'No, I don't know Holly, but she wrote to me... told me you were in trouble.'

'It was none of her business, damn her! How did she find you?' Cathy's voice was tense with frustration. 'Even I didn't know where you were.'

'She used her initiative, I guess. Tracked me down. She knew my Buddhist name and my birth name, which you must have told her.'

'Did I, did I tell her?' Cathy asked herself, running her fingers through her hair. 'Yes, I suppose I did... but I never expected... ' Cathy glanced at him briefly, her thoughts and emotions in turmoil. 'Oh, for God's sake sit down.'

'I'd prefer not to while you're pacing around,' he said quietly.

'How did she know which monastery to write to?'

'I've no idea, but from her letter I suspect she wrote to more than one.'

'She's meddling in things that have nothing to do with her! I didn't give her permission to find you, contact you. You'd gone! I was trying to make a life for myself... and Jason.' She turned and faced him for a moment, her face tense with anguish. She drew in her breath, went to the window and looked out. 'I'd been wondering who the stranger was, standing in the shadows.'

'I guess I've lost my touch: you saw me.'

'Why so covert? Why didn't you tell me you were here? It's not nice, you know, skulking.'

Blake hesitated for a moment. 'I didn't know if I'd be welcome. I didn't know what your circumstances were. I needed time.'

'So, you lurk around on a pavement, stalking me.' She raised her voice in annoyance. 'And then... don't deny it... you break into the flat, and completely violate my privacy by planting bugs. That's a terrible thing to do, isn't it? Do you deny it?'

He put his hands up in surrender. 'I don't deny it.'

Cathy stood up straight, hands on hips, and glared at him. 'You call yourself a Buddhist monk, living according to the precepts, non-violence, honesty, right action and so on, but you're nothing but a fraud.'

'Do you want me to defend myself?'

'Defend the indefensible?'

'I had to determine your situation before I acted.' He took a deep breath and thrust his hands deep into his jeans pockets. 'Six and a half years have passed, Cathy. For all I knew the letter might have been a hoax.'

'But you came back, to check me out.'

'Yes.'

'It's six and a half years since I last saw you... It's all too much, a shock. Oh God!' She put her hands to her heart.

'It must be; I'm sorry. It's not a good way to meet again, not the way I would have chosen. Perhaps you need some space... I could come back another time... whatever's best for you... '

'No, no, of course not. Don't leave. I didn't mean I'm not pleased to see you... I just need to adjust... it's a lot to take in.' She waved her hand in front of her face as if feeling the heat.

'I know, me too.' He looked at her inquiringly. 'Just because I'm a Buddhist monk doesn't mean I don't feel, Cathy… or that I have forgotten.'

'It's been a long time…'

'Yes.'

She stood for a moment and looked over at him.

'But seeing you now, it doesn't feel that long.' Their eyes locked and she whispered, 'It feels like just yesterday, somehow.'

'Yes it does, for me too,' he said quietly. 'Time is an illusion.'

'It's a long way to come.' She sighed and looked up at the ceiling briefly. 'Have you been back before?'

'Yes.'

'But you never thought of getting in touch?'

'No, I thought it better not to.'

'Why, because you weren't interested?'

'No, because I thought you might have moved on.'

'And you didn't want to disturb me.'

'Yes.'

'But this was different.'

'Yes, I was prepared to take the chance. I didn't want you to be in trouble.'

'So you rescued me.'

'I wouldn't put it quite like that.'

'I don't need bloody rescuing, I'm an independent woman. I don't need your or anybody's help.'

'It didn't seem like that to me.'

With both hands gripping the back of the armchair, she glared at him.

'I wasn't in trouble, I could have handled him.'

'But you still called for me.'

She fought back tears of frustration.

'Yes,' she said angrily. 'Oh God, I'm so confused… '

'You've been manipulated. I'm sorry. Simon Scott is a

wife-beater and a scheming conman.'

'He is?' Her eyes welled with tears and she sat down on the armrest of the sofa.

'Cathy, what do you know about him, his history, his background?'

'All I know is he had his own business and he was scammed by his business partner. He lost his house, his wife and a lot of money.'

'This business partner, Derek Prowder, you mean?'

'Yes, I knew his name was Derek, but I didn't know his surname.'

'It's a neat little story, isn't it, and cleverly near the truth but twisted; it's not quite right.'

'What do you mean?'

'Simon's business partner, Derek, remortgaged his house to finance expansion of the business.' Blake paced about. 'Simon had no part in raising funds. Simon was abusing his wife Amy and she left him, moving in with Derek. For months before this, on the quiet, Simon was slowly embezzling money from the business, which collapsed. As a result Derek lost his house. Simon was caught and in order to avoid a prison sentence he paid back a lot of the money; he'd spent much of it already and his mother, Margaret, picked up a hefty chunk of the bill.'

'The bastard! His mother bailed him out?'

'There's a murky history there as well. She inherited a large sum from her aunt, but there were questions raised at the time about the validity of her aunt's will.'

'It might have been fraud?'

'Possibly.'

'How do you know all this?'

'I checked his background, then his mother's. When I discovered it was dubious I decided you were most probably in trouble, especially considering Amy, so I set up some microphones to keep you safe.'

Cathy gulped and sat quietly for a moment.

'How did you do it, Blake? How did you find out?'

Blake shrugged. 'Cathy, there are ways, if you know how... '

'I know.' She looked away. 'You've had the training... ' She stared him in the eye. 'I won't ask.'

'I'm sorry you got mixed up with him.'

'He'll be back, Blake, and you won't be here,' she said, looking up at him.

'No, he's not coming back,' said Blake, quietly but confidently. There was something about his expression that made her heart miss a beat.

'Oh God. What, you haven't killed him, have you?'

Blake caught his breath. 'No, I don't do that anymore. I just frightened him off.'

Cathy took a long, hard look at him.

'You're still a spy, with military expertise, aren't you, Blake, really? Not a Buddhist monk at all. You'll always be a spy first.'

Blake sighed, looking wounded. 'I will defend you, even if it means breaking my precepts.'

They were silent for a few moments. Blake went over to the photograph of Jason on a set of drawers, gently picked it up and looked at it.

'That's a very nice son you have.'

'Yes.' Cathy looked away.

'How old is Jason, five, six?' he asked quietly.

Cathy studied him closely, then answered in a whisper, 'Six'.

'Six years old. When was he born?'

'2nd April 1981.'

'2nd April,' said Blake, almost inaudibly. 'Jason calls him Uncle Simon, not Daddy?'

'Yes. But how do you know that?'

'I heard it through the microphones…'

'Of course you did.'

'But you married him.'

'Yes, I wanted a man in my life. For Jason's sake. He needed a father.'

'I see.'

Cathy got up and stood near him.

'You weren't here, you were lost to me,' she said quietly.

'I was never lost. You could have told me.' He held her gaze steadily. She shivered, his unfathomable dark eyes penetrating into her depths; she was vacant, open, unprotected. 'He's my son, isn't he?'

Cathy nodded.

Blake took a deep breath and put the photo back.

'Then why... why not tell me?'

'You had already gone.'

'You could have found me; I left my address with Mr Dunn.'

'It was too late. You were gone, on your damned spiritual quest. I wasn't going to try and drag you back, to bother you.'

'Bother me!' Blake grasped the set of drawers the photo was propped up on.

Cathy put her finger to her lips. 'Shh... ' she said, 'Jason will hear.'

'Really, Cathy.' He shook his head in exasperation.

'I'm sorry. I thought I was doing the right thing.'

Blake breathed deeply and steadily.

'You could have found out, when you knew I had a son... you found out everything else... why didn't you?'

Blake said quietly, 'It was difficult... I didn't want to know.'

'I see... '

'He's a lovely boy. You're doing a great job.'

'I've done my best... but...' she pursed her lips and

tried to suppress the spasm in her voice, 'but there hasn't been a day that's gone by, Blake, when I haven't wanted you in my life...' Tears gushed from her eyes. 'I missed you so much,' she burst out.

Blake took her in his arms; she clutched at him, feeling his warmth, his strength, the subtlety of his aroma, not of anything in particular, just of him, a smell she remembered so well. She collapsed into him; she felt safe, supported, home at last.

'Mummy,' said Jason as he burst into the living room, wearing his pyjamas. He stopped and stared at them.

'Me... me too.' He rushed towards them and Blake lifted him into his arms. All three hugged in a loving embrace.

.

CHAPTER 36

Six months later. March 1988
An Lac Monastery, Delat, Vietnam

'I like living here with the monks,' said Jason as he carefully put on his canvas shoe. One shoe on, he looked up at Cathy. 'But why can't we live together with Daddy in his kuti? He's got the biggest kuti in the whole place.' He looked towards Blake's kuti and pointed, frowning. 'I want to live with Daddy.'

'Jason, we have discussed this before.'

'But why, Mummy?'

Cathy bit her lip. 'It's because he's important.'

'Why is he important?'

'Because he's the man in charge, the Abbot. So he needs to live on his own.'

'I don't want to live on my own.'

'No, neither do I, darling.'

Jason cocked his head and frowned. 'Why don't any other Mummies live here?'

Cathy sighed. 'Er, well... because most monks don't have any children.'

'Why not?'

'Oh Jason, look... you're going to be late for school if you don't hurry.' Cathy helped him with the other shoe. 'Get your satchel, let's go.'

Jason plucked the satchel off its hook on the bamboo wall. 'Ready,' he said.

Cathy took his hand as they went down the kuti steps and walked with him to the entrance of the monastery. There was dew on the coarse, thick grass that bordered the curving path. The sun rose in a clear sky and there was a fresh smell of frangipani. She hurried him to the bus stop a few yards away. As they arrived the rickety bus pulled up, on time for once. Jason sat in a seat by the window, Cathy next to him in the aisle. There was a mother with a baby in a sling sitting quietly on the bus, a frail old man with a stick who firmly grasped the back of the seat in front, and a woman carrying a goat on her lap. Once the bus was on the open road it passed vibrant green rice fields and banana plantations where men and women with bent backs and palm leaf conical hats tended their crops. In the distance an enormous buffalo pulled a plough. The motor roared as the bus swayed from side to side over the potholed road. As they came in to On Dang village the fields gave way to red-roofed stone buildings, a winding street and colourful gardens. People swarmed around going about their business. Looking out of the window, there was a cacophony of noise, hustle and bustle. There were street-sellers serving hot food to passers-by, who slurped down their soup or noodles and hurried off. Cathy saw a man walking along, two live chickens trussed up with thin rope draped over his shoulder. Suddenly the rope came loose and the chickens fell to the ground, squawking. They ran in front of the bus with the man chasing them. The bus driver slammed on the brakes, just missing the trio, and swore at them through the open window. Soon afterwards the bus pulled up outside a clump of squat wooden buildings; on one hung a sign in Vietnamese, 'On Dang Primary School'. Children passed through the entrance.

'Here we are', said Cathy and led Jason out of the bus. At the school gate she kissed him swiftly on the cheek.

'Bye, Mum.' Jason skipped into the school yard, a flat space of bare earth; in a corner were some simple wooden climbing frames.

As usual, Cathy watched anxiously. A huddle of children formed around Jason, who was still a novelty.

Most of the children walked to school from nearby hamlets, the kindly headmaster, Mr Kyon, had told her on the first day. Jason was the only one who travelled by bus. And he was the only European child in the whole school. Not only that, but the only one living in the monastery, with his mother. From time to time the monks took in boys who had been orphaned, but one living there together with his mother was quite exceptional. Mr Kyon's tone had not been punitive but inquisitive. 'Of course, European, Western way of life different from Vietnam, we traditional way of life here,' he'd said and nodded repetitively. 'We not question Ajahn Annando's decisions, he respected Abbott.' She had the impression they thought her a special kind of charity case as some of the other mothers went out of their way to offer her food and clothes. She respectfully declined, trying not to cause offence.

When Cathy got back to the kuti that she shared with Jason, she swept the porch clean, made the beds, hand-washed some clothes in the sink in the female guesthouse and hung them up to dry. Later, carrying a basket of lychees she'd picked earlier that morning, she went to the kitchen adjacent to the sala, the meeting hall, and helped the local village women prepare and serve the midday meal to the monks. Each day different villagers came to donate food on a weekly rota. After a chant and blessings, the villagers stood in the courtyard in a row behind their pots and pans, ladles in their hands, ready to offer their food to each monk as he came up to them with his bowl. Each villager had brought food they had sourced and prepared themselves in the monastery kitchen. In the heat of the afternoon Cathy had a short siesta then pulled out her books and studied Vietnamese until it was time to collect Jason from school. In the bus on the way home they practised speaking Vietnamese to each other, and Cathy was pleased to see that Jason was more fluent than she. It was a regular day, following the same routine.

When Blake had suggested that they come and live with him in the monastery Cathy had been apprehensive. She had wondered how it would be as a woman among so many monks, but now being here and seeing that there were many female guests and village women coming and going every day to help or just to visit the temple and meditate, she felt much more at ease. But then there was no one she could confide in and few who spoke English. Some of the monks did, but they did not seek her company. She didn't kid herself; she had known what she was coming to and what it would be like, Blake had been very clear, but it was hard, harder than she had imagined. She was with him, but not quite with him, living nearby in this artificial way. And there was never any privacy; it was forbidden for him to be left alone with a woman. When she did talk to him, with others nearby, it was only about practical things. She longed to be intimate, in her thoughts and physically. Sometimes her isolation felt like a physical pain, but at the same time she didn't want to be anywhere else.

* * *

Late one night Cathy felt she could stand it no more; she stole out of her hut and silently made her way to Blake's kuti. Never having been allowed inside, she was intrigued about what it might be like, but cautious as she knew she was breaking the rules. At the top of the few steps she slowly parted the curtain of beads, crept through the portal and scanned the interior. The small space led to one room lit by the light of the moon, which shone through a window covered with a close-meshed insect screen. As her eyes adjusted to the light she could just make out a simple table and chair, a bamboo chest and a bed on a wooden frame. Blake was in the bed, asleep. Quietly she knelt beside him. She could hear his breathing, slow and regular. He was bare-chested, wearing a pair of loose cotton trousers. Cathy stayed still, watching, her heart beating a little fast, as his chest rose and fell. She put out her hand, and keeping it one or two centimetres above him, she felt the warmth of his body. She leaned closer and breathed in deeply, smelling the maleness of him. Blake moved in his sleep and turned on his side, facing her.

'Blake,' she whispered, put her hand on his chest, and rocked him gently. 'Blake,' she said, louder. He stirred and opened his eyes. 'Blake, it's me, Cathy.'

He took a deep breath and stirred; his eyes blinked open. He looked bleary-eyed at her.

'Cathy, what are you doing here?' He was suddenly alert, sitting up. 'What is it? Is there something wrong? Is it Jason?'

'No, he's fine.'

He sighed with relief and flopped back on the bed.

'Then why are you here?'

Cathy was silent for a moment, gathering her thoughts. Blake twisted towards her and, lying on his side, rested his hand on his cheek.

'What's the problem, Cathy?'

'There is no problem.'

'Well, obviously something's wrong or you wouldn't be here.' In the light of the moon she could make out the concern in his expression and the light reflected in his eyes.

'I miss you.'

'You miss me.'

'Yes.'

Blake lay back and sighed. 'Cathy, you see me every day. I'm never far away. You're as near to me as I can make you.'

'You may be physically near but it feels hundreds of miles away.'

'This is not the time or place for this discussion.'

'There is no other time and place. I never see you alone.'

'You knew what you were coming to; we've discussed it over and over, this is the only way it will work.'

She sniffed a little.

'I long to be held by you, touched by you. I love you.'

Blake swung his legs off the bed, sat on its edge and took her hands in his. 'You know that's not possible.'

'Please, Blake, no one will know. I want us to be together... physically... I need it. I need you.'

'Cathy, you knew what I was offering you.'

'Yes, I did, but it's not enough. Every day I see you and long for you. Just this once, please.' Back and forth, she stroked his arm and shoulder, put her arms around him and hugged him. Blake gently eased her away.

'I can't. It's impossible.'

'The only thing that's impossible is to love you and not be with you.' Softly, she began to cry.

'I'm sorry; I know it's very hard.'

'Leave this life, Blake, for me and Jason.'

Blake gently shook his head.

'I'm the Abbot; I've got fifty monks relying on me.'

'They can do without you, Jason and I can't.' Her breath was on his cheek and she pressed her lips on his.

Resistance failing, Blake responded, kissing her passionately, feeling the stirrings in his groin. Cathy pressed herself against him, but he held her back.

'No, Cathy,' he said. 'I feel compassion, love and responsibility, for you and for Jason, of course I do, but that's all that I can offer.' His voice was tight, his breathing deep and fast.

Flickers of torchlight shone through the window and

they heard soft footsteps approaching.

'Who's that?' asked Cathy, her heart thumping.

'Shhh...' The footsteps faded away. 'That's Venerable Candavaro. He does a circuit of the monastery every night. He'll be back in about ten minutes or so after he's been down to the main gate. Sometimes he pops in to see me.'

'Comes in?'

'Yes, I don't know why, he never mentions anything specific. If I'm awake we exchange a few words. I think he just checks that I'm still alive.'

'Then I'll go,' said Cathy.

'You'd better. I'll discuss this with you another time... when I can.'

'Thank you, my love. I'll be waiting.'

She slipped out quietly and went back to her hut.

CHAPTER 37

'How long has she been missing?' Blake asked the novice monk, in Vietnamese.

'Since dawn.'

Blake looked at his watch. 'What time exactly?'

'At 6.30 this morning Jason was found on the path, calling for his mother. Venerable Papanamanda saw her heading towards the paddy fields at sunrise. About 5.00am.'

'That's not unusual. She sometimes goes that way early to collect lychees. But she's always back before 6 o'clock to take Jason to school. Where is he now?'

'He's in the sala. Venerable Sunnido is with him.'

'Has Jason been told about his mother?'

'No, I don't think so.'

'Quite right at this stage, but why wasn't I told earlier?'

'You were in solitary meditation; we didn't want to disturb you.'

Blake stiffened.

'That is a mistake. I must always be disturbed when there is an emergency in the monastery.'

'We didn't know if it was an emergency.'

'Someone goes missing, of course it's an emergency.'

'Yes, Banti.'

'Send out a search party, scour the area. Use every monk, novice, visitor, everyone. Send them out in twos or threes. When she's found, bring her straight here. I'll go to Jason.'

'Yes, Banti.' Anagarika Succasito, the novice monk, backed away with his head bowed, quietly wondering why Annando appeared so disturbed. He thought maybe there was something he had done to offend him. He had never seen Annando that way before.

* * *

'Banti, what is it?' asked Jason, looking up at his father. The boy sat comfortably in the lotus position, back straight, on a circular cushion on the floor. 'Why do you keep walking up and down and looking out of the window?'

'Nothing important, just something on my mind.' Blake smiled kindly at his son.

'I don't understand. You are always mindful, but you aren't today. Does your mind make you jumpy like a monkey?'

'It can. Being aware of your own agitated mind is a mindfulness practice in itself. Awareness is the important thing. Watch the monkey of the mind but do not try to smother it.'

'Is Mummy taking me to school?'

'We'll see.'

Jason turned his attention back to his book and carefully turned the pages. 'I like this story.'

'Which one is that?'

'The one about the Buddha and the elephant.'

'Your favourite.'

'Yes.'

There were urgent shouts in the distance. Looking out he saw four monks coming into the monastery carrying someone on a stretcher. He took a deep breath. They walked carefully but quickly. Blake glanced down at Jason, now absorbed in the book and reading quietly to himself, his fingers moving under each word as he read it. Blake watched the monks until they went out of sight behind some buildings. Then he squatted down and put a reassuring hand on Jason's shoulder.

'I need to meet some bhikkhus; you'll be OK for a few moments on your own, won't you?'

Jason looked up, nodded and went back to his book.

Breathing heavily, Blake hurried to the medical room, now bustling as monks crowded around; as he pushed his way in the monks stood back, giving him space. Cathy lay on a bed, her skin pale. One leg of her trousers had been cut open, exposing several large red weals on her shin. Her calf was a deep shade of pink and swollen. Blake put the palm of his hand on Cathy's forehead. Her skin felt cold and clammy.

Venerable Sunnido smeared the wound with ointment.

'What happened?' Blake asked him urgently.

'Snake bite.'

'How do you know?'

'These are the symptoms.'

Blake drew his breath in. 'What snake?

'Difficult to tell.' Sunnido avoided his gaze. 'Could be the Monocellate Cobra... she has more than one bite.'

'What can we do?' asked Blake.

'Better if monks wait outside,' said Sunnido looking quickly around the room. 'I have injected her with anti-venom.'

The other monks bowed and quietly left the room. Blake felt his heart thump; he grabbed hold of Cathy's hand and leant over her.

'I'm here, Cathy,' he whispered reassuringly, 'hold on.'

Sunnido's expression said everything; gravity was etched in every furrow and crease of his face.

'We did not find her fast enough.'

Blake stroked her cheek and held her cold, unresponsive hand. He looked up pleadingly at Sunnido.

'What else? There must be something else we can give her...' Blake's voice began to crack.

Sunnido shook his head. 'Nothing. Not while she is

unconscious like this.'

Blake rocked her gently in his arms. 'Wake up, my Cathy, we need to give you medicine, you need to sit up.'

Cathy groaned quietly, her breathing shallow and laboured.

'Is she in pain?'

'She is not conscious of any sensations.'

'We need to get her to hospital. I'll send someone for transport.'

Sunnido didn't respond; he looked Blake in the eye grimly without speaking. Annando is behaving very strangely, he thought. He feels attachment to this woman as I always thought. I'm sure he is suffering.

Blake called to the monks who clustered around the doorway, silently listening and waiting.

'We need transport to Su Chi hospital,' he said, 'run, quick as you can, every moment counts.'

After a quick deliberation three monks ran towards the sala.

'Cathy, wake up,' said Blake urgently, gently rubbing her hand. 'She's so cold, so limp... so unresponsive.'

He looked Sunnido in the eye.

'It is the venom of the cobra. It is this snake, I am sure. It's in her system now,' said Sunnido.

'What's the prognosis?' asked Blake.

Sunnido bent down and dabbed some more ointment on Cathy's wound, sighed and wiped his brow with the back of his hand.

'This isn't good, is it?' said Blake.

Sunnido avoided his gaze; he didn't answer.

'The prognosis?' insisted Blake with a tremor in his voice.

Sunnido looked up at Blake and slowly shook his head.

'No!' Blake felt his throat constrict and his legs began to go weak; a wave of heat overwhelmed him. He wrapped his arms around Cathy and pulled her to him, looking into her face. He felt her cold, clammy skin against his. 'Don't leave,' he said. 'Be strong.'

Cathy moaned slightly and partially opened her eyes. They didn't focus; slowly she went limp and slipped away.

* * *

Two days later

With his father holding his hand, Jason crept quietly and respectfully into the shrine room where his mother's body was laid out on a plinth covered with a yellow cloth. She was dressed in traditional Vietnamese clothes, a long white shirt and short-sleeved silk top. Surrounding her was a plethora of colourful flowers. Jason had never seen his mother in such clothes before, although her face he recognised well. Yes, this definitely was his Mummy.

He looked at his father and whispered, 'Why is Mummy wearing those clothes?'

'The village women have dressed her in traditional clothes. It's what they do when someone dies.'

Surrounding her body, and facing towards her, were five monks; three lay women sat on the floor. They were silent, some meditating with their eyes closed, some sitting. A village woman smiled kindly at Jason and beckoned him nearer. He recognised her as a friendly lady. Jason looked up at his father.

Annando nodded encouragingly and squatted beside Jason. 'Go to her, don't be afraid.'

Jason went to the woman, who patted the empty space on the floor beside her with her hand, her face serene and loving. Jason sat down. Close up, the flowers were strongly fragrant. It was an extraordinary experience, something he'd never done before. Instinctively, Jason reached out and touched his mother's arm. Flinching at how cold it was, he withdrew it quickly. Noticing, the woman put her hand on Cathy's arm and stroked it gently and reverently, all the while smiling at Jason.

Jason felt strangely peaceful. His beloved mother was a curious sight, so still, so cold. Daddy explained that Mummy was not coming back, but then Mummy had said his Daddy was dead and that hadn't been true. He had cried a lot, but Daddy had been with him all the time and the monks and lay people had been so kind. Daddy had said it would be good for Jason to see Mummy and to know for himself that she was dead and how peaceful she was.

Eventually, he got up and stood next to his father.

'Why did the snake have to bite her?'

Annando smiled kindly at his son and, after some time, he said, 'This is the way things are.'

'Why did Mummy have to die?'

'All is impermanent. We never know what will come next. Only this moment is real.'

'I'm glad I've seen her,' said Jason contemplatively.

'Yes, it is good,' replied Annando gently.

'How long will she be here?'

'Another few days. There will always be monks around her. You can visit whenever you wish. Would you like that?'

'Yes, please.'

'If you want me to be with you, or to be on your own with Mummy, just ask.'

Jason nodded.

'I am here for you, as long as there is breath in my body. We all are, everyone here in the monastery, the Sangha, we are all your family.'

Jason looked up at his father and smiled. They quietly made their way out of the shrine room.

* * *

Six years later

Jason, dressed in brown robes, crossed the grassy knoll, climbed the steps of the sala and entered through the porch. He took off his sandals, laid them neatly against the wall and went inside. Annando sat alone, cross-legged in the middle of the floor, meditating. Jason spread his square seating cloth neatly on the ground in front of his father and knelt on it. He bowed, then sat in the lotus position on the cloth. Annando opened his eyes and smiled tenderly at his son.

'Annando,' said Jason, 'I am making progress with my practice. I am more mindful every day, I am mindful of everything I do.'

Annando's eyes sparkled, and he smiled knowingly. 'And at which side of the porch did you leave your sandals when you entered the sala, to the right or to the left?'

Jason thought for a moment, put his finger on his lip and sighed. 'I cannot exactly remember.' He bowed his head in regret. 'I've got a long way to go, haven't I?'

'We all have, Dhammaloka, my son. This is a lifetime's work. And this is the contradiction: although it is a lifetime's work, the only moment you can realise the truth is now.'

Dhammaloka put his palms together in front of him and bowed his head respectfully at his father's teaching.

'Yes, awareness of the present moment is the only true reality. I will contemplate this daily until the next full moon.'

'And all the full moons until the end of your time here on earth.'

Dhammaloka bowed respectfully, 'Yes, Ajahn.'